BLOODTHIRST

BLOODTHIRST

MARK RONSON

C

CENTURY

LONDON MELBOURNE AUCKLAND JOHANNESBURG

First published in Great Britain in 1979 by
Hamlyn Paperbacks
This hardcover edition published in 1986 by
Century Hutchinson Ltd
Brookmount House, 62–65 Chandos Place
London WC2N 4NW

Century Hutchinson Australia Pty Ltd
PO Box 496, 16–22 Church Street, Hawthorn, Victoria 3122, Australia

Century Hutchinson New Zealand Limited
PO Box 40–086, Glenfield, Auckland 10, New Zealand

Century Hutchinson South Africa (Pty) Ltd
PO Box 337, Bergvlei 2012, South Africa

ISBN 0 7126 9562 1

Reprinted in Great Britain by
WBC Print Ltd, Bristol

...for the life of all flesh is
the blood thereof: whosoever eateth
it shall be cut off.

—Leviticus chapter 18 verse 14

For Robert

A DREAM WITHIN A DREAM

The rosy dream seemed endless; an awareness which was neither life nor death, without knowledge of self yet with dim remembrance of a dream dreamed before. Occasionally there was a presentiment that somewhere along the artery of time a new dream would be dreamed.

At other times it became strangely sensual as the dreamer floated liquescent through hall after damask hall with the stirrings of transient memory . . . fantastical forms glimpsed through a ruby darkly, pulsations of dread rippling kaleidoscopic walls, a thirst for something forgotten but still desired, crimson flashes of hate which slowly lapsed back into the calm of the dream.

With this calm came vague comprehension that without life there cannot be death; the inkling that a cycle must complete and the dreamer's time would come again.

I

Sheet lightning shimmered over the eastern horizon, reminding Heinrich Köbler of artillery flashes. Perhaps the main body of the retreating Panzers were still embattled with the Ivans but if so it had little interest for him. Corporal Bauer often said the war was only ten square metres round you and, as usual, the corporal was right. Heinrich remembered seeing a Mark VI tank wrecked by an explosive shell. From a safe distance he had watched a crew member try to haul his flaming body through the hatch. The agony of the frantic puppet meant nothing to him; yet when a 'Stalin organ' fountained white and orange so close the blast sent him reeling, his veteran bowels voided like those of a recruit in his first bombardment.

Corporal Bauer knew all right! That sausage butcher from Hamburg who, in keeping with the traditional joke, was sometimes called Hummel, was a professional survivor. Hummel or not, that morning he had saved his fleeing squad when he repaired a staff car which had been strafed by a Stormvik. A dead officer with lightning flash insignia had been slumped over the wheel. His companions had bolted and Heinrich hoped the Ivans or the Hungarian partisans had caught the bastards. That would teach them war was something more than strutting in black uniforms and booting Jews and Gypsies about. . . .

As he plodded at the head of exhausted men Corporal Hans Bauer enjoyed thinking back to the Mercedes. It proved what a useless lot these jumped-up officers were when it came to anything practical. They had abandoned their car, yet he only had to lift the bonnet to find the damage caused by a random bullet. He shortened a broken lead, reconnected it and they were bouncing along as though they were all wearing oak leaves. That was one in the eye for The Professor. . . .

Klaus Wankel – known without affection as The Professor – kept his pink-rimmed eyes on the bulging back of Corporal Bauer. To remain fat, when the hungry nightmare of the East European offensive had reduced the army to shambling skeletons, was a tribute to his uncanny power of self-preservation. For the thousandth time Klaus wished Bauer would stop using him as his butt.

Of course, he knew it was class prejudice. In the long gone days of peace Corporal Bauer sweated long hours in stinking surroundings while Klaus Wankel carried his teacher's brief-case leisurely in Bad Kreuznach, the spa town of nightingales and roses. Bauer had the contempt of his class for the bourgeoisie; and this was increased by an irritating habit the Professor had never been able to control – that of imparting information.

Mentally he tried to excuse himself that it was because his mind had always been so active. Was it his fault if he had an intellectual approach to life? Yet it placed a barrier between him and the rest of the squad. For example, when the order had come for the withdrawal he had given an impromptu lecture on Napoleon's retreat from Moscow, pointing out that only a third of the army managed to return to their French Fatherland. Corporal Bauer had shouted: 'Shut up, Professor, or I'll lose my boot up your arse.'

Klaus still felt shame about this. He knew it had been very wrong to lower morale even further – if that were possible – and he had desperately wanted to rectify his error, even though he could not alter the fact he had been a professional

2

man while Hans Bauer had the soul of a peasant, and in this dreadful freezing country it was only peasants who stood a chance. Yet part of his mind still pictured the ghosts of the *Grande Armée* watching from snow-sheeted firs the repetition of a once invincible force collapsing before what the Russians called Comrade Winter. . . .

Little Werner Hase reeled as he tried to keep up with the small party. God alone knew where they were, or what had happened to the Panzer brigade. Everything had become chaos after Ivan's artillery had caught them in the valley, while Stormviks howled through it like death angels. Finding the abandoned staff car had saved them. They had escaped the bombardment but had lost the column, supposing there still was a column. Corporal Bauer had driven it until there was no more petrol and now all he could do was lead them west, west to the Fatherland, west to Werner's beloved Bavaria and his beloved Lotte in Schwangau. In his fantasies – especially when Red Army guns threw tall snow columns about them – he imagined being in an enormous feather bed with Lotte, melting into her generous warmth and finding refuge from the world.

Through his fatigue he felt a sudden spasm of hate for the Führer and the slogans which once sounded glorious – 'Strength through joy' and 'My blood for the Fatherland'.

It started with parades which brought tears of pride and ended in this bloody shambles. It had been the greatest confidence trick of all time. Ludwig had been right, poor misunderstood King Ludwig of Bavaria who had died mysteriously on the shore of Starnberg Lake, a lunatic in the eyes of the world. He built beautiful palaces instead of buying glory on distant battlefields with the lives of his subjects.

Dear God, thought Werner, I'd give my soul to walk the forest path round Neuschwanstein once more and listen to the thunder of the cataract. . . .

3

'Halt!' Corporal Bauer ordered.

The five soldiers closed about him.

'We'd better eat and rest,' he growled. 'Up there looks all right to me.'

Their eyes followed his sausage finger to where, in the spectral glow of snowlight, they saw a ruined church surrounded by a coppice of shattered tombstones.

Bauer looked it over with an experienced eye. Its walls were blown outwards, indicating a direct hit, and the graveyard was pocked with small craters, but in a far corner a low mausoleum remained intact. Surprisingly an allegorical statue was still in place above an arch from which bronze doors had been wrenched by the blast.

'In here, lads.'

'But, corporal, it's a grave,' protested Heinrich Köbler. 'It'd be bad luck . . .'

'*Mensch*! You should know by now to fear the living, not the dead,' retorted Bauer. 'In there we can boil coffee and the partisans won't see our fire.'

Excited by the thought of a warm drink in their bellies the soldiers stumbled down steps into the tomb. The corporal lit a stump of candle, making shadows caper grotesquely. They were in a large marble vault lined with massive stone shelves on which rested ancient coffins. Bauer held his candle close to one, its flame reflecting on a dark panel of carved wood.

'In those days corpses of aristocrats were better housed than living workers,' he muttered in disgust.

Werner Hase made a little pyramid of the dry sticks which had made his greatcoat pockets bulge. Another man unhooked a pan from his pack while a third produced a tin of ersatz coffee. Soon flames from the small fire illuminated the worn faces of the Germans and the tiered sarcophagi behind them.

4

The corporal put down his Nagan machine-pistol and held up a flask.

'I've got a treat for you bastards,' he grinned. 'What do you say to some schnapps in your rot-gut coffee?'

'Hummel! Hummel!' laughed Heinrich Köbler. 'Where did you get that, Hummel?'

'It's by courtesy of the captain we found in the Mercedes,' Bauer answered. 'His SS mates were in such a hurry they forgot to take it off him.'

'Swine – those SS,' Werner Hase muttered as he crouched over the burning sticks. 'It's because of what they've done in our name the Reds crucify prisoners.' He shuddered. To him the Russians were devils rather than flesh-and-blood enemies. Oh yes, he'd seen plenty of dead Ivans frozen stiff with bandages round their feet instead of socks, but only once had he actually seen the living enemy – white shapes slinking through trees like wolves. From his trench he'd opened up with his MG38, but he never knew if he'd hit any of the phantoms. No one dared to leave the emplacement to see.

Water began to bubble in the pan. Candle in hand, Bauer prowled to the far end of the chamber.

'One of these fancy boxes has been knocked down,' he called. 'Looks like there's a kid inside it.'

Two of the party joined him. In falling from a slab of red stone the lid had been displaced. In the trembling light they could see the small figure wrapped in a yellowed shroud, but showing no signs of decomposition.

'He's kept well,' the corporal commented. He peered at the metal plate on the lid, but it was too tarnished for him to read name or date.

'I'll have this,' he muttered and prised it from the ancient wood with the point of his bayonet. 'I'll bet you it's silver.'

Klaus Wankel gazed with fascination at the body. It was

5

about the same size as the boys he had taught before he was mobilized, but none of his pupils had shown such dignity of feature even in repose. The boy's eyes were closed, the face gaunt but serene.

Heinrich Köbler said: 'Funny he hasn't rotted. I thought they turned into dust in the end.'

'It is unusual, yes,' answered Klaus Wankel, and before he could check himself he had launched into his role of The Professor.

'The superstitious Catholic Church regards the lack of decomposition as a sign of holiness,' he declared. 'It was a factor always considered in the canonization of saints. But in East Europe the Orthodox Church took the opposite view. A body which did not decompose was regarded as something evil. For example, in Greece graves were often desecrated because the ignorant feared ...'

The sentence was lost in the staccato din of a submachine gun reverberating in the confined space. Flashes from its muzzle illuminated the mausoleum like a strobe light. From his crouched position Corporal Bauer saw his companions assume warped postures of death, their screams obliterated by the noise of the gun which winked like an orange eye at the vault entrance.

The burst ended and Bauer realized he was the only one still alive. His ability to survive had not deserted him. Because he had been kneeling at the coffin the swathe of death had passed over him. By the firelight the corporal saw three figures in camouflage white. As they stepped into the chamber they reminded him of monks in white cowls.

Dropping the piece of metal into the open coffin, he straightened up and held his hands shoulder high.

'*Kamerad*! *Kamerad*!' he said, and grinned.

The three came close.

'*Zhal potratit patron na etu svoloch*!' said the one with the submachine gun, leaning against a coffin.

'Fellow workers,' said Corporal Bauer. 'I am *kamerad*, a worker like you. I spit on the bosses who make workers kill each other. You must understand that. . . .'

A burly figure stepped forward and looked into the German's stubbled face. He smiled, exposing a row of metal teeth, then raised a knife and placed the razor sharp point against Bauer's neck, just below the corner of the jawbone. He made a neat downwards cut.

As the blood from the nick trickled under his collar Corporal Hans Bauer knew from his peacetime experience what was to come. How often had he done the same to a pig dangling by its hind legs from a chain!

The enemy turned the knife tip in the incision, then moved his arm with skilful strength. The corporal's last thought, as he felt his life gush away through his gaping throat, was that his executioner really was a fellow worker – the Ivan had been a butcher.

The body buckled and collapsed across the open casket. The three Russians frisked the corpses, grunted with satisfaction when they found the schnapps and were soon retracing their steps along the tracks which had led them to their prey. Sheet lightning shimmered over the eastern horizon. Inside the sepulchre the stillness was broken only by the soft sound of blood dripping into the coffin of the long dead child.

2

Anyone who claims not to believe in mental telepathy cannot have worked in a hospital. The currents of information which sweep such establishments without visible means of communication are nothing short of miraculous. So it was one dull, late-winter afternoon at the London Hospital for Diseases of the Nervous System. In Fleming Ward Sister ordered a snap tidy-up campaign exactly seven minutes before Matron phoned a warning that Sir Henry Beresford was on his way with a very special 'tourist' party.

Nurses scurried from bed to bed straightening coverlets, clearing locker-tops, parting old men's hair and wresting chromium-plated 'bottles' from incontinent males who wanted to keep them within easy reach. It was made clear that the bedpan service would be discontinued until Sir Henry departed, and God help any patient blasphemous enough to feel a call of nature while the great man was in the vicinity.

The ward was immaculate when he hove into view, white coat flying dramatically, at the head of his visitors. Elegant, wealthy and Edwardian in style, he was one of the two top neurologists in Britain. The other also worked at the hospital, but was the antithesis of the tall Sir Henry with his beautifully barbered steel hair, trim moustache and grey aristocratic eyes.

The visitors were the executive board of a charitable foundation which, having been left half a million pounds by a conscience-stricken property tycoon, were seeking a worth-

8

while cause in which to invest. Behind walked several doctors to supply tactful answers when required.

Nurses stiffened to attention as the party entered the ward, then relaxed as it was led straight to a side room.

'Ladies and gentlemen,' said Sir Henry as they ranged themselves opposite a row of beds in which several children were asleep, 'the aim in such a specialized institution as this is threefold: to care for the sick, to train specialists and carry out research. This work falls in the latter class, and Dr Pilgrim is carrying it out through the aid of a Lord Foundation fellowship. I am sure he is best fitted to explain it.'

'Here we are investigating the causes of narcolepsy,' Dr Pilgrim said with an easy smile. He was of middle height with a well-proportioned frame and a straight-nosed face which, at unguarded moments, tended to be tight-lipped. Heavy brows overshadowed thoughtful hazel eyes and his only physical concession to the fact his next birthday would be his 30th was threads of grey in his long dark hair.

'Briefly narcolepsy is a rare condition in which the patient suffers from sudden attacks of sleep,' he continued. 'In some cases it is a tendency to doze off at unexpected moments, in more severe ones the victim will become unconscious in the middle of speaking a sentence. The length of these unnatural sleeps also vary, but they can be very distressing. No narcoleptic can drive a car or work at a machine or do anything in which an unexpected loss of consciousness might injure him or those about him. It can carry social stigma where the disease is not properly understood – family members, social acquaintances and workmates may regard the victim as being idle or lazy. Narcolepsy is so rare hardly any research projects have been carried out on it. Indeed, apart from being thought to originate from a damaged hypothalamus, nothing of value is known, and certainly there is no effective treatment as yet.

'These children are severe cases from all over Britain. Their periods of sleep are often very long, almost comatose at times – I say "almost" because the difference between sleep and coma is that in the latter case the patient cannot be roused. These children can be awakened with difficulty. Now what we are attempting here . . .'

'What *you* are attempting, Dr Pilgrim,' interjected Sir Henry with modesty at first deceiving. With experience gained through a tough career, it was his rule to be included in a project only when it was proving successful.

'What I am doing is to catalogue every symptom. Periods of sleep and wakefulness are monitored, together with all associated bodily functions and brain activity which is tested regularly by encephalograms. This data is processed to enable a pattern to be formed, and it is through the building up of this pattern I hope to narrow down the likely causes of the disorder. My greatest problem is not having instant access to a computer.'

'Thank you, Dr Pilgrim,' Sir Henry beamed. 'Now, ladies and gentlemen, perhaps you would care to see our surgical suites.'

As the party approached the operating theatres on a lower floor, a trim, fair-haired sister walked briskly down the corridor. As she passed the group Dr Pilgrim dropped his ballpoint and, as the visitors moved on, he and the girl bent together to pick it up.

'Tomorrow okay?' he hissed.

'Yes,' she whispered back, then straightening said formally: 'Your pen, Dr Pilgrim.'

'Well, I hope old Beresford was pleased with this afternoon's exercise,' Dr Peter Pilgrim remarked to Dr Tudor Owens as they rested their elbows on the bar of the Mason's Arms, the local pub used by the medical staff of the nearby hospital.

'You were bloody marvellous, boy-o,' his companion grinned. 'When you brought in that bit about the need for a computer, I think the old bastard could have kissed you. He's been after one for years, indeed yes. He's potty about electronic medicine.'

Tudor Owens was balding, florid and genial. The loves of his life were rugby and its associated booze-ups (he played half-back for one of the London-Welsh teams), his red sports car (known as The Haemorrhage to his colleagues) and a succession of willing nurses, in that order. The young neurologist's only fear was that he might fall in love in an unguarded moment and lose his glorious bachelorhood.

'We could certainly use a computer,' said Peter. 'It'd make my life a lot easier.'

'Again please, Helen,' ordered Tudor. 'You don't have much to complain of. You're on a good number here. Make it spin out, boy-o. The secret of success is always to make everything appear difficult. But you're doing all right, I see.'

'How do you mean?'

'With that French bird who picked up your pen. You have a loud whisper. Old Beresford must have heard you making your date. Well, good luck. There's a lot of betting on how soon you'll make it.'

'Good God!'

'You can never keep a secret in a hospital, boy-o. But there's an extra lot of speculation about you and Anne-Marie Clair. Because she's cold and French, she's been nicknamed *La Glaçonne* by the nurses. So go to it, Peter. We all want to see if you can crack the ice, and there's a lot of money riding on you. But be discreet, you know Matron's view about doctors and nurses even in these enlightened and permissive times. . . .'

'Coming from you, that's the best joke yet.'

'The sin is only in being found out. By the way, I hear we

can expect a visiting fireman from Scandinavia soon, a top neuro by the name of Stromberg. He's set up a fancy clinic somewhere in Finland, and now he wants to have a look round our shop. If you ask me he's talent scouting, but old Beresford is probably pleased. One sympathetic voice closer to the Nobel Prize, and if his new radiation technique works out he could be in the running. . . .'

The talk became technical, but Peter's mind was back with the girl he had encountered in the corridor. He could understand a certain amount of jealousy from her less endowed colleagues, but it had never occurred to him that there was anything about her to suggest an icicle. Perhaps he had been allowed to see her from a different standpoint to everyone else; perhaps he was much luckier than he had realized.

Lionel Tedworth was a hospital orderly whose plump smile was bland and often kindly, a mask that rarely slipped. He lived alone in a chintzy bedsitter and for five years, after abandoning his dream of becoming an actor, he had worked at the London Hospital for Diseases of the Nervous System.

This evening he walked with his usual briskness into the large entrance hall which had recently been modernized to give the impression of an airline hotel foyer. But this failed to disguise the basic hospital atmosphere. Many fear its antiseptic tang, an odour which conjures for them visions of unprotected flesh at the mercy of strange chemicals or honed steel, or ultimate horror behind gay curtained screens. To Lionel it was the scent of security. The tidal rhythms of the hospital, its warmth, its efficient order in a disordered world, soothed him.

The orderly took the large-caged lift up to Fleming Ward where he changed into a white coat before walking down the central passage to Sister's office. The ward was part of the modern wing and, instead of being an old-fashioned dormitory, it was really a wide corridor off which were rooms of varying sizes which accommodated patients according to their sex, condition and treatment.

He arrived exactly on time for the twelve-hour night shift at Sister's neat desk, to be followed by Staff Nurse Hoskins, a cheerful, well-scrubbed girl from Somerset whose passion in life had been bell-ringing.

'Good evening, Staff,' said Sister. 'Good evening, Lionel.' She looked down at the record book in the glow of the green-shaded lamp. 'It's been a quiet day. Mr Hayes is still on the drip and I think you'd better give Mrs Shapiro phenobarb tonight, she's had a rather disturbed day. The leucotomy came back from theatre a couple of hours ago and Nurse Wakeling is already on the post-op vigil. . . .'

Lionel listened to the routine report with contentment. Although orderlies were officially only manual helpers, he had absorbed some medical knowledge and when the nurses were rushed off their feet was often trusted to do more than was in his official line of duty.

'There are two new patients,' concluded Sister. 'A Mrs Davidson in for observations, suspected aneurism, and down for a CFS test. And there's a new addition to the narco-leptics, a little Scandinavian girl called Britt. Her father brought her to London for a consultation and she went into coma. You'd better read the report, Staff, it looks a bit odd to me. Dr Pilgrim wants an EEG done as soon as possible so you'd better take her down, Lionel.'

After further instructions Sister departed and Lionel wheeled a trolley to a room at the end of the ward. In the eerie light of a blue bulb dolls and teddy bears kept watch over the narcoleptic children, who were as unaware as their toys.

In the bed nearest the door lay a beautiful child. Silver blonde hair cascaded over the pillow on either side of her face, her rosy lips were slightly smiling as her breast moved regularly beneath the crimson coverlet. Lionel remembered with sudden vividness an illustration of the Sleeping Beauty from a fairy tale book which had fascinated him in childhood.

'She's a pretty one,' Nurse Hoskins said. 'Such a shame!'

Lionel agreed automatically as, with the ease of constant practice, he and the nurse lifted her slender body on to the trolley. Then the child, still locked in her trance, was wheeled to the lift. The aged operator made clucking sounds through his toothless gums when he saw her. Soon the trolley was squeaking into the Electroencephalographic Department. An efficient young woman in a green coat deftly attached small electrodes, smeared with special conductive cream, to key points on the child's skull.

'See she doesn't move,' she instructed. 'Even the winking of an eye will show up on the EEG graph.'

'She's not likely to move, miss,' retorted Lionel in a tone which indicated he had been longer at the London than she. 'The patient's suffering from some kind of cataplexy.'

The technician adjusted the eight cables which led Medusa-like from the girl's head to the EEG apparatus, checked the indicator lights on the console and flicked a switch. There was an electronic hum and an endless roll of graphed paper slid under eight styli behind a perspex panel.

An electroencephalographic machine works by recording electrical impulses which arise in the human brain. Even if the patient is unconscious the automatic mental reflexes which control the body's pulse rate, breathing, temperature and so on are strong enough to be picked up by the ultra-sensitive electrodes. These impulses are amplified and cause the styli to move to and fro over the paper according to the strength of the signals.

In a healthy person the signals from both lobes of the brain are identical, thus the four styli reflecting the impulses of the left lobe should make the same flowing pattern as the four mirroring the right. Where there is a tumour or other lesion there is a change in the pattern and experienced neurosurgeons can frequently locate the position of the disorder by studying yards of ruled paper covered with the styli's spider tracks.

Lionel looked from the patient's peaceful face to the styli resting on the moving paper like wire fingers. They should have been zig-zagging. Instead they remained still, with eight perfectly straight lines flowing from their inky points.

'You're not getting a reading,' he reported.

'I can see that,' retorted the technician. She halted the moving paper and inspected the cables which ran from Britt's head. All were correctly connected to the terminals.

The process was repeated, and again the result was eight straight lines.

'It was working all right an hour ago,' said the technician almost apologetically. 'Are you sure your patient's all right – you'd only get a reading like that from a corpse.'

Lionel felt the throb of Britt's pulse.

'She's alive all right,' he said. 'Slow but steady. If you ask me it's your machine that's dead.'

The EEG operator pushed her fingers wearily through her hair.

'Probably something very simple,' she said, 'but I won't waste any more time with it now. I should've gone home ages ago. Orderly, move the trolley over to the stand-by machine.'

The trolley was wheeled over to an identical machine.

'We should get it this time,' the technician said as a ruby eye winked and the dials flickered into activity. Lionel watched as the new roll of paper began to move under the styli, but again only eight rectilineal marks showed on the travelling paper.

'Still not working,' Lionel announced.

'It must be your patient,' the EEG girl replied.

'She's only in a coma, she's not dead.'

'According to our two latest, most sophisticated machines she's not alive either. It's impossible that both can go on the blink at the identical moment. I'll get the electronics engineer to check them out tomorrow, but meanwhile I suggest you get Dr Pilgrim to have a good look at her. It seems to me there is no activity there at all.'

'She can't be neither alive nor dead,' Lionel objected, releasing the trolley brake.

The technician collected the strips of graphed paper, neatly concertina-ed them and laid them on the rug covering Britt.

'You'd better let Dr Pilgrim see those just to prove what I'm saying,' she said. 'Perhaps it's a brand new disease. I ran tests on the other narcoleptics and they all responded.'

The trolley squeaked back to the room where the narcoleptic children lay deep in their unnatural trances. After Staff Nurse Hoskins learned of the EEG result she instructed Lionel to check Britt's pulse and respiration every twenty minutes.

'I'm sure it's some fault in that damn gadget,' she said, 'but we'd better be on the safe side until Dr Pilgrim sees her. If he can't get a proper reading he'll probably want a ventriculogram done.'

Lionel smiled secretly, hoping this would upset Dr Pilgrim's programme. He did not like Dr Pilgrim because he was not decorous enough. Lionel had a great sense of propriety when it came to hospital life, believing doctors should behave with traditional dignity. When Dr Pilgrim first came into Fleming Ward wearing a turtle-necked sweater he had been quite scandalized.

At ten-thirty Lionel made a routine ward check while the

16

nurses busied themselves with the leucotomy patient who was sinking.

He stepped into one door and heard the 'hiss-swish hiss-swish' of a respiratory machine. In the old days such breathing appliances had been frighteningly termed 'iron lungs'. From coffin-like tanks encasing victims of paralysis, they had evolved to light plastic casings which fitted over the patient's trunk with airtight seals allowing the head and limbs to protrude. A pumping machine connected by a tube to the casing rhythmically changed the pressure thus forcing the patient's lungs to expand and contract. Here the patient was a young woman who had suffered almost total paralysis following a car crash.

The fact that Jennifer had been a promising tennis player made her case all the more tragic. Lionel saw tears glisten in the eyes of the most hardened nurses on the dreadful morning her fiancé sent a note breaking off their engagement. Hysterically she had begged them to switch off the motor which kept her alive.

'Everything all right, Jennifer?' Lionel asked.

'Thank you,' she answered in a whisper. 'I just can't sleep tonight. Sometimes I wonder if the room is haunted.'

'That's a funny idea to have.'

'I suppose scores – perhaps even hundreds of people have died in this room since the hospital was built. Surely there must be some ghosts around.'

'It's too antiseptic for ghosts,' said Lionel. 'You need ruined castles and ancient graveyards and places like that to make ghosts feel at home.'

The girl gave an odd laugh, distorted by the pulsation of the breathing apparatus.

'I must be getting morbid. I know it's stupid, but for the last few hours I've felt there's something bad . . . something

17

evil . . . close to me. My granny used to be psychic. They say you take after your grandparents, don't they?'

'I wouldn't worry about it,' said Lionel in his special pacificatory voice. 'With the greatest respect to your old gran, she probably saw things after a couple of gins too many.'

'I suppose you can't help having funny notions when you're caged up in a machine,' she said with sudden bitterness. 'Life isn't real any more.'

In the dim office Lionel looked at the luminous hands of his watch. It was two o'clock in the morning, the period known to the staff as the 'witch hour' when, according to hospital superstition and statistical fact, most patients die.

He yawned and walked softly to the bed of the little Swedish girl. In the pale beam of his torch she looked unnaturally beautiful with her spun silver-gold hair framing small exquisite features. As he counted her respiration her eyelids fluttered and he found himself gazing into ice blue eyes. She murmured something in Swedish, and then gave him a slow smile which dissolved the solemnity of her grave expression.

He bent closer.

A strange, dangerous and breath-catching urge came over him – the temptation to softly kiss the slightly parted lips of the Sleeping Beauty. This was immediately followed by a steadying twinge of guilt that he should feel such an unprofessional emotion. Kissing little girls had once brought trouble to Lionel which for years he had determinedly pushed into the attics of his memory, yet the urge grew and slowly he lowered his head. With a look of secret knowledge, the girl raised hers.

Two arms clasped the orderly round the neck and Britt pulled his face close to hers with unexpected strength.

God, if Staff should walk in! he thought in a panic. But the fear was submerged under a rush of emotion as he felt

18

Britt's lips on his face, soft and moist as rose petals after rain.

'*Törstig*,' she whispered. '*Törstig, älskara.*'

Her lips explored his cheek, lingering on his mouth and then creeping down his jawline until he felt their warmth on his neck.

He was filled with an erotic sensation of dissolving into a dream of indescribable pleasure. Next instant the dream became a nightmare. The flower mouth at his throat opened and a savage pain seared him, causing him to straighten up with an ungainly reflex action. Britt's arms were tightly round his neck, clinging with the desperation of a drowning swimmer, and the only effect of his convulsed movement was to drag her out of bed.

Still she clasped him as they crashed to the floor. Still her teeth remained deep in his palpitating throat while she frantically swallowed the blood flowing into her mouth.

3

The taxi drew up outside the Villa Dei Cesari and the driver concluded his indignation about the Black September hijack and became a man of business. In the lamplight the Thames Embankment gleamed wetly. Anne-Marie Clair dashed for the canopied restaurant entrance while Peter Pilgrim settled the fare. He joined her in the foyer with prismatic raindrops in his hair just as she handed her cloak to the toga-ed attendant. She faced him with a smile.

'Do I look all right, Dr Pilgrim?'

He gazed back at her and thought how good she did look. Not only did she have a generous mouth (a feature that always found a response with him), violet eyes and delicate bone structure, but an expression of unusual mobility. But perhaps her most striking feature was the pale gold hair which fell on each side of her face to shoulder level.

'You're absolutely fine,' he answered, and felt a warm touch of pride that he was her escort in this sophisticated place.

The head waiter hovered.

'There's a table booked in the name of Pilgrim,' Peter said. 'Sorry we're a little late.'

'This way, sir.' The couple were led into the main body of the restaurant, across a sunken dance floor and up to a gallery where through large windows they could see the Thames flowing fast and mysterious under the slanting rain.

'Is there something on your mind?' the French girl asked as they seated themselves.

He nodded and ordered a large whisky from the wine waiter. He downed it quickly while Anne-Marie sipped a Campari soda.

'A little Swedish girl has just joined my group,' he explained. 'The extraordinary thing is that we can't get an EEG reading on her. We tried different machines last night and today, and they all remained negative. It was as though we were trying to get a response from a corpse.'

'But that's impossible.'

'Impossible but true. Not that she is corpse-like. She woke up for a few seconds and managed to bite the Fleming orderly last night.'

Anne-Marie giggled.

'If it was that Tedworth creature I think she has good sense. He gives me the creeps with his funny looks. . . .'

'Funny looks or not, he will certainly remember Britt,' said Peter. 'Anyway, I've had a frustrating day, trying tests without any joy, and I'm sick of shop.'

He smiled at her suddenly and said: 'Happy birthday, Anne-Marie.' From his pocket he took a flat paper packet. 'For you,' he added.

'*Merci beaucoup*,' she responded in an imitation of stage French. She untied the string and found the gift to be a large double buckle of antique silverwork.

'Oh, Peter, how marvellous. But how did you know it was my birthday?'

'Through bribery,' he admitted. 'A large box of chocolates to Miss Potts, and she got it for me from your file.'

'I don't think I approve of that, but many thanks, dear Peter. Now I shall be able to hold my own with your English nurses.'

She was referring to the hospital custom of girls with SRN

status wearing ornate clasps on the broad black belts which encircled their navy pinstripe uniforms nicknamed 'butchers' aprons'. This dress, said to date back to the days of Florence Nightingale, was sacrosanct in the tradition of the hospital, and the antique buckles were the only hint of individuality allowed.

'I found it on a stall in Portobello Road.'

She was about to kiss him when a waiter materialized to take their order. When they were eating they saw the lights of a vessel heading downstream from a berth by the Battersea power station. Its port light threw a brief red streak on the black water.

'Ships that pass in the night, is it not so?' mused Anne-Marie.

'Are we ships that pass in the night?' Peter asked.

She gave a little shrug.

'I do not know,' she answered slowly. 'You know I return to Paris after my course ends . . .'

'That's still some time away,' he interrupted. 'And I've got a few plans before that happens. Look, spring is almost here. How about coming up to Northumberland with me in a couple of weeks? My father lives up there in a cottage he's modernized, and it's about time I visited the old boy. You'd love it up there, and I know he'd make you very welcome.'

'Sounds nice,' she said. 'I shall come with you. I think I have a long weekend coming up.'

'And I'm due for some leave, so it'll be okay. I'll write to Dad. Despite the fact he's terribly busy on his current book, I worry in case he's lonely.'

'That's settled then,' Anne-Marie said. 'But I hope I'll see you before then, and by that I don't mean glimpses of your white coat vanishing down a corridor.'

'Don't worry,' Peter chuckled. 'There's a new play that has had some good reviews. . . .' And they began working out when the hospital schedules would leave them free for their next outing. Then the meal was over and they were dancing.

'Do you want to make some money?' Peter whispered when the music became low and old fashioned.

'*Argent* I can always use,' Anne-Marie laughed.

'Well, there's some betting going on for which you have inside information. . . .' And he repeated what Tudor Owens had said about the hospital punters.

'Dr Owens is a dreadful man,' Anne-Marie declared, but Peter saw her eyes light with amusement.

A cheerful West Indian nurse ushered August Hallström into the reception office where Peter Pilgrim waited to interview him. Britt's father was a tall man with a long and narrow head. Only in the strands of blond hair, brushed forward over a balding brow, did he show any resemblance to his daughter. Peter wondered that such an ungainly man should have fathered such a fairy child, yet when he smiled he had a shy charm.

'Good morning, doctor,' he said with a slight bow. 'I believe you are interested in my daughter's case.' His English was flat-toned but grammatically perfect.

'Sit down, Mr Hallström,' said Peter. 'Nurse, please bring us some coffee. Yes, I am very interested in Britt's condition. I'm already studying a group of narcoleptic children, and your little girl seems to fall into that category. But before we discuss her case, I'd like to know exactly what happened.'

'Last summer I took my wife and Britt for a holiday in Lapland,' he explained. 'We left Norrköping, where I have a construction business, in our Volvo and drove north up to Finnmark where we visited Hammerfest. Britt was very excited because it is the most northerly town in the world.

'We camped out everywhere, and it was a good holiday.

23

But on the return journey, near a village called Kaamanen, it happened. Do you know Lapland, doctor?'

Peter shook his head.

'It is a marvellous country. The last piece of natural unspoilt land in Europe with forests which stretch hundreds of kilometres in every direction. It is in the marshes the mosquitoes breed in summer. They are the real terrors of the north because when they attack they attack in thousands. They will get round a reindeer and worry it so much it will run through the trees until it falls over a cliff or dashes itself against a rock. There have been cases of travellers needing blood transfusions after they have been sucked by these thirsty insects.

'Of course we had our nets for sleeping. I did not know then it could be dangerous in daytime. I parked by the roadside and lit the Primus to make coffee. Britt could see water shining through the trees and off she went. We did not realize we were near a mosquito swamp.

'Suddenly I heard Britt scream. I ran in the direction of the sound, and I saw a black cloud of them round her. They are not the little mosquitoes you have in England. These were great black monsters. No matter what she did they swirled round her, settling on every centimetre of exposed skin and sucking her blood. They crawled within her clothes, into her ears and up her nostrils.

'She was hysterical, beating the air about her and running. I shouted for her to stop, but she just raced madly through the trees with me running after her. It was like following a moving black pillar.

'Then she vanished from sight. I ran up and found that in her panic she had run over a steep bank by a stream. She was lying half in the water. In her fall she had gashed her head and her arm on sharp stones. I picked her up and made my way back to the Volvo. It was difficult because by now the

24

mosquitoes were round me. I put her in the back seat with my wife and we drove off.

'My child was in a bad way. I think she was unconscious but it was hard to tell. Her face was so swollen the eyes were completely closed. Soon I had to let my wife take the wheel because my eyes were closing too.

'Luckily a timber truck came along the road, and my wife stopped it. The driver told her there was a medical centre nearby, and when we reached it Britt was well looked after. She had the gash in her arm stitched, and was given a transfusion for loss of blood, and shock. At first they were afraid of concussion, but after three days we were allowed to continue our journey home.

'There she began to complain of being drowsy all the time. She began to go into what you might call trances. Once she actually went to sleep riding her bicycle.'

'That's a symptom of narcolepsy all right,' Peter said.

'I thought it was due to her fall. I still do. I took her to a hospital in Stockholm and there they did all the tests, but they could find nothing.'

'Did you bring her notes?'

'Yes.' August Hallström opened his briefcase and produced a black folder of papers. He handed them across the desk.

'The top ones are in Swedish language,' he explained. 'Under them are translations I had done by a medical translator.'

'You are very thorough,' said Peter, leafing through the pages. The Jamaican nurse brought in coffee and beamed at Britt's father.

'Finally, I took her to a top specialist,' he continued. 'He said I should bring her to London, so I flew over with Britt. I was going to make an appointment as a private patient, but just after we had landed she collapsed. We were in the taxi,

25

so I had the chauffeur bring her straight here, because this is the hospital Dr Stromberg recommended. He said it was the best in the world for nervous disorders. His letter of introduction is there.'

'Mr Hallström, were there any other symptoms your daughter showed after the mosquito accident?' Peter asked.

It seemed a troubled look came into the Swede's pale eyes.

Peter continued carefully: 'What I mean, was there anything else? For example, did she have any personality changes?'

The father rubbed his hand wearily across his face.

'Of course the accident had an effect on her,' he said. 'Afterwards she could not stand the sight of a mosquito.'

'You must be frank with me if I am to be of any help,' Peter said. 'Last night I regret to say your daughter woke up and attacked one of the hospital staff. To be exact, she bit him badly.'

'Oh no!'

'Has it happened before?'

Hallström nodded, eyes cast down.

'Anything else?'

'Yes, doctor. She seemed to develop sexually more than was normal for her age. I do not think she has had intercourse yet, but she suddenly seemed interested in men – *men*, not boys. And in young women, too. She became over-affectionate with them.'

He paused wearily. 'It was a young student, the son of a neighbour, whom she attacked in Sweden. He was in our garden. Suddenly she put her arms round him and tried to bite, but he threw her off. He was scared in case we should think he was . . . you understand? I know because my wife saw it all. And then there was her kitten.'

'What about her kitten?'

26

Hallström raised his hands and let them fall weakly.

'She cut its head off . . . with scissors.'

He paused again.

'I cannot explain it. Before her accident she loved that kitten. She has changed, yet most of the time she seems sweeter than ever. Do you think there could be brain damage?'

'I can't say yet,' Peter answered. 'But there is one thing to remember, Mr Hallström. This abnormal behaviour is sure to be connected with the accident. Do not blame her, blame whatever it is that has happened to her. Meanwhile we will do everything in our power to discover what it is and correct it.'

'You are a kind man, doctor,' said Hallström, standing up. 'I was beginning to fear my Britt was becoming a monster – a monster with the face of an angel.'

> '*Tell us, pray what devil*
> *This melancholy is, which can transform*
> *Man into monsters,*'

Peter quoted.

'Please?' Hallström said from the door.

'Lines from a seventeenth-century English writer called John Ford,' Peter explained. 'Now I suggest you see the almoner, Mr Hallström. There are some papers you must sign.'

The Swede gave his tight little bow and left the room.

'He's sure sad, that man,' remarked the Jamaican nurse as she cleared away the coffee cups.

When Peter met Anne-Marie that evening for supper she chided him for being preoccupied.

'You know our pact not to get bogged down with hospital gossip,' he answered.

27

'If you are worried, Peter-Pierre . . .'

He told her about Britt's EEG results, followed by the attack on Lionel Tedworth.

'For some reason – perhaps through shock – he went into a coma himself,' he continued. 'On a hunch I had him taken down for an EEG. Believe it or not, the same reading came up for him as Britt. In other words, there was no reaction at all – he was neither alive nor dead!'

'That's ridiculous,' Anne-Marie declared. 'You're too imaginative. You get it from your father. It's obvious the machines are faulty.'

'They're working okay today.'

'Coincidence!'

He nodded and smiled at her.

'You're probably right. Now, what are we going to eat?'

Britt surfaced from her dream. The room was illuminated by a forty-watt bulb with a blue shade. By its light she saw nurse slumped over the table, asleep with her head on her arms. She smiled and climbed out of her bed. Life had become so strange, she hardly knew when she was awake and when she was dreaming. What was she doing here? And where was Daddy? And where was that nice man who made her so happy when she kissed him?

The other children were asleep in their beds ranged round the room. Britt felt she loved them all, but it was unfair they hardly ever woke up at the same time as she. She went from bed to bed, looking down on them. If only they were her brothers and sisters! She yearned to make them part of her dreams. She would kiss them just as she had kissed that nice man who had tasted so good.

She bent over a small boy who lay with his arms above his head on the pillow. His hair was a mass of ringlets which earned him the nickname of Curlytop among the staff.

28

'I do love you, I do love you,' murmured Britt as she put her face close to his. For a moment the narcoleptic child's face became a rictus of pain, but the trance held him and he relaxed. Joyfully Britt straightened up, the tip of her tongue caressing her lips. She went to the next bed. . . .

Nurse continued to sleep, unaffected by the restless stirring of her charges. Finally Britt returned to her bed and smiled up at a well-worn Teddy. Now they would be her brothers and sisters and share her dreams.

It was another hour before nurse opened her eyes, guiltily looked at her watch and began to check the pulse and respiration of her patients. It was then she saw the teeth marks.

4

The same Friday morning that Peter Pilgrim and Anne-Marie began their drive to Northumberland, a journalist named Holly Archer was summoned by her editor. His office had white carpeting and chrome furniture with black leather. On the dove-grey wall behind his rosewood desk was a large baize board to which were pinned the latest *Revue* campaign posters. They reflected the editorial content of a weekly paper which, despite stiff competition and the explosion of colour television, still sold over a million copies . . . 'Is SHE Prince Charles's Miss Right?' – 'Spot Our Man on the Run' – 'Confessions of a Love Drug Smuggler' – 'Knit this Exciting Sweater'.

As Holly entered, mentally contrasting the opulence with the drab olive-green rooms where journalists yawned at typewriters chained to their desks, the editor rose with his famous courtesy and indicated an armchair so low it made the occupant look up to him.

'No thanks,' said Holly brightly. 'I'll sit over here.' She perched on the arm of an avant-garde sofa. The editor nodded good-naturedly and reseated himself. He fixed her with a fatherly smile which she knew from bitter experience was the mask of the hardest taskmaster she had ever served. During her three years on *Revue* her preoccupation had been meeting his challenges.

It had been a favourite trick of his to think up a headline and then make her find a story to fit it. After a year of these gruelling tests she was promoted to feature-writer and her pay almost doubled. Apart from old Bob Wilson who did crime, she was now regarded as the best staff writer, a position she fought to hold by a high quota of stories which followed *Revue*'s unofficial dictum of 'Blood, Sex and Royalty'.

'What have you coming up for us this week?' the editor asked.

Holly knew he was well aware of what each member of his staff was working on through his morning consultations with the features editor, but she answered dutifully: 'I'm doing a beat-up on cell therapy rejuvenation.'

'Are you?' said the editor, whose mind worked in headlines. ' "Blood Boosts Banish Old Age Blues", eh?'

'Something like that,' Holly admitted.

'That can keep, but if there's anything genuine in it you might give me a memo – our chairman would be interested. Do you feel like a trip to Copenhagen?'

'Not that!' wailed Holly. 'Circulation dipping again?'

'Put it this way, it could do with a bit of cell therapy – sex cell therapy, ha ha ha!'

'What can I do on the porno scene which hasn't been done already?' demanded Holly, turning her palms outward.

'Ah!' said the editor with a chilling smile. 'That's for *you* to find out. Look at it from the woman's angle – ha ha ha! Try and get close to one of the live action performers and get her story. How about "Public Copulation Saved My Marriage"? I've been on to the promotion boys and you'll get a TV commercial out of it.'

'That should be good. As long as it has a couple of full frontals and my name read out loud enough to shock my old mum. . . .'

'Your old mum should be very proud of you,' said the editor soothingly. 'You know you're one of the best human-interest writers we've ever had, so be a good girl and pop over this afternoon. Betty's fixing the flight tickets now, and we've jacked up a local freelance photographer called Christian Christiansen to do the picture coverage. Do a good job and I promise you a story in the south of France. Okay?'

'Bribery will get you anywhere,' Holly grinned.

As Holly strapped herself into the seat of the SAS DC9 at Heathrow Airport, she was suddenly amused at her previous annoyance over this assignment. Three years ago when, wide-eyed after a boring stint on a provincial newspaper, she had been given a month's trial on *Revue*, she would have been delirious at the thought of flying off to foreign cities at short notice. Now she was used to it. She had her own flat in Hampstead and drove an ageing but still very fast Aston Martin which had been resprayed sulphur. Her life was made up of smart parties, PR receptions where cocktails circulated with Fleet Street slander, and suppers with celebrities at the expensive restaurants.

But she knew that on the Street one had to keep running to stand still. She was only as good as her last story, and she sometimes woke up with the fear her talent was running out.

She thought wryly it was natural for the editor to give her this assignment because of her brash image. Yet in one respect she was the least qualified of all the *Revue* staff to cover the erotic nightlife of the Danish capital. Holly had a secret she would have hated any of her colleagues to guess – she was still a virgin.

She had worked with too much intensity to be interested in an emotional relationship with any of the men she had met, even though many had been fascinating. She could not accept the idea of giving her virginity in some casual encounter.

Holly felt that this was probably wrong in the liberated 'seventies, and that perhaps she ought to see a psychiatrist,

32

though maybe it was the drive of sublimation which was responsible for her present high-powered position. If that was the price for a full and amusing life, it wasn't too high and it wasn't a state that had to be permanent.

She summoned a hostess, ordered a large gin and tonic and settled back to study photostats of cuttings from the newspaper morgue on the Scandinavian sex scene. Already the intro to her story was forming in her lively mind: *'Once upon a time Copenhagen was a quaint old back-drop for Hans Christian Andersen fairy tales. Its most typical postcard showed the statue of his Little Mermaid. Today Copenhagen is the sex-fun centre of the world, and it's a wonder the Little Mermaid . . .'*

The old man raised his eyes from the stainless steel sink for the hundredth time and let them follow the road which wound up the fell between parallel dry-stone walls. Peter had written that he would arrive in time for lunch, and his father was determined to prove to him – and this new girl he was bringing – that he was still able to look after himself. There was *coq au vin* in the oven at low heat, and leek soup, his Border speciality, filled the kitchen with a delicious smell.

Ambrose Pilgrim finished cleaning his cooking implements, wiped his hands on a strip of kitchen roll and looked south up the fellside again. A metallic blue Citroën appeared against the skyline, then swooped down towards the cottage. Ambrose opened the door and the cold air burned his nostrils after the warmth of his Aga stove.

With a scrunch of soft tyres the car halted by the cottage and Peter climbed out and ran towards his father.

'Dad!'

'Hello, old chap. You're just in time for lunch. Where did you get such a magnificent car?'

Peter grinned. 'I must admit it's slightly second hand, but

she's a beauty. A Pallas. But I must introduce you to Anne-Marie. . . .' But he did not move. And the French girl in the front seat of the Citroën, which was now settling itself like some colossal insect tired after its race from London, did not move either. She had the tact to let father and son make their greeting alone. The young doctor scanned his father's face with a professional glance, looking for minute signs which would indicate his state of health.

'I'm all right, Peter,' laughed Ambrose. 'Pretty fit in fact. It's the Border air.'

Peter turned and opened the car door. Ambrose watched the girl climb out, lithe and graceful. Under her white ski sweater her breasts were full for one so slim.

'Father, I want you to meet Anne-Marie Clair,' said Peter, holding her by the hand. 'Anne-Marie, this is my old dad, Ambrose Pilgrim, of not unknown literary fame.' Ambrose felt her hand cool and firm.

'I am happy to meet you, my dear. Do come in out of the cold. There's coffee glugging away in the Russell Hobbs. You must need some after such a long drive.'

Anne-Marie surveyed the bright kitchen with approval. It was orderly without being prim, and she was not surprised to learn that in his time Ambrose had done a lot of sailing. He looked after his home as though he were on a boat, apart from his study, which later Anne-Marie discovered to be a confusion of books and papers massed round tape recorders and an IBM typewriter.

Now she was studying Ambrose as he busied himself with the coffee, while Peter complimented him on the improvements he had made to the cottage. She was happy Peter's father had turned out to be this kindly lean man with a finely wrinkled face and mane of white hair. Peter would look like this when he grew old, and she was glad.

'Come into the lounge,' Ambrose said, leading the way

34

with a tray. 'How do you like the new furniture? Last time I was in London I went berserk in John Lewis's, but it seems to work out now it's assembled.'

Smiling, he handed them steaming cups.

'Have a good trip up?'

'It was very good,' said Anne-Marie, lounging in a huge swivel chair. 'It took five hours coming on the M1 and then the M6. But I slept most of the time.'

'Anne-Marie had to work very late in theatre last night,' Peter explained. 'But we won't talk about that. We have a pact to keep off subjects medical this weekend.'

'I'm glad,' said Ambrose with an exaggerated shudder. 'I dare not think of what horrors are perpetrated in that hospital of yours. Now excuse me, I have a culinary operation to perform on the chicken.'

'He's lovely, your father,' whispered Anne-Marie as the old man retired to the kitchen. 'In that navy sweater he's just my idea of a writer.'

'This electric cooker is too complicated,' came Ambrose's voice through the doorway. 'So many dials. With all these knobs and dials I sometimes think I'm at a NASA control console with ten seconds to zero . . . Ah, I think we have lift-off.'

'Smells delicious,' Anne-Marie called encouragingly.

'Dad only came here a couple of years ago,' Peter explained. 'It was derelict when he bought it.'

'Do you like Northumberland after London?' she asked Ambrose when he returned.

'I found the city lost a lot of its attraction for me when Peter's mother died,' he answered. 'And I get more work done here.'

Anne-Marie looked down at her slender hands. She knew little of the family history. Peter led her to a window while Ambrose bustled about with plates. To the north, under a delicate water colour sky, they saw a distant line of blue hills; nearer at hand the ground sloped to a valley dissected by stone walls. At the bottom a small tarn gleamed like a burnished coin in the cold sunshine.

'I'd forgotten the marvellous views you have,' Peter exclaimed.

'Before you only saw it in winter. It is very different in spring but autumn is the golden time for the Border. We have a very late summer – note that "we". I'm becoming a native. Now get your bags in and take Anne-Marie to her room. I think the room nearest the top of the stairs is the nicest for a young lady.'

Peter thought: It's the room farthest from his, so if we were to spend the night together there'll be no embarrassment.

Soon Anne-Marie returned to her big chair and curled up.

'I am pleased to meet you, not only because you are Peter's papa, but once I read one of your books – in French. After that I became a fan.'

Ambrose gave a little nod to accept the compliment but did not dwell on it.

'Which part of France do you come from?' he asked.

'Paris – St Cloud.'

'Of course, I should have recognized a Parisienne.'

'Not pure Parisienne. My father is an engineer there, but Mama comes from the south, so I spent much of my childhood near Arles.'

'Then you must know the Camargue.'

'I adore it. When my course ends I'm having a holiday there. I want Peter to come with me for the Gypsy festival.'

Lunch was a great success. Even Anne-Marie, with her French palate, had to admit that Ambrose was a fair cook. The Hockheimer Peter had brought in a crate full of assorted bottles for his father was followed by Hine brandy, putting them at ease and lessening the need to talk.

'Have you heard from Julia?' Peter asked as he lolled before the log fire. 'I only get a letter when she wants advice on x-raying some ancient skull.'

'She's fine,' Ambrose replied. 'Still in Abu Sabbah. I worry because she's close to the trouble zone, but it doesn't seem to bother her. She believes she's on to the tomb of a priest of the Eighteenth Dynasty. Sometimes I wish she'd meet some nice fellow and settle.'

'Not really!' exclaimed Anne-Marie. 'To have a daughter who is an archaeologist should make you proud.' .

Ambrose smiled, and said: 'I suppose if I have given anything to my children it is the gift of curiosity. For Julia it is delving into the remote past, for Peter it is probing into the human mind.'

'Literally,' said Anne-Marie. 'I can tell you he wields a deft scalpel.'

'Remember our pact,' laughed Peter.

'Indeed, even the thought of blood makes me feel faint,' Ambrose said.

'Yet you have written about some pretty gory happenings,' said Peter. He turned to Anne-Marie. 'The Battle of Bosworth made my father's name and fortune. That, and the later historical books, enabled Julia to become an archaeologist and financed my psychiatry studies after I'd got my general qualifications.' He raised his glass. 'Here's to the noble dead whom Ambrose Pilgrim resurrects so successfully and profitably.'

'I just try to bring a bit of life back into history,' said Ambrose modestly. 'When I was a schoolmaster I was shocked to find that such a fascinating subject was usually the dullest on the curriculum. It has been a popular trend to dehumanize it, to see it as social movements and statistics. I have merely put the flesh and blood back on the dry bones in my books.'

After some discussion about the book Ambrose was currently working on, Anne-Marie announced she was still rather tired and went upstairs, partly to sleep and partly to allow father and son to be alone together.

'About Anne-Marie . . .' Peter began as the two men went into the kitchen to do the washing up.

'I think you have chosen right this time,' Ambrose said. 'She's good-hearted, she has humour and she's very alive. A fine person, and I sincerely hope it works out.'

'Early days yet,' Peter said quickly. 'But she has proved to me that I can have feelings again. When Marian left me my world ended. Because of my training I was supposed to have some understanding of human emotions, to know all was to forgive all – but such precepts no longer made sense. Life was empty and desperate, and I felt that my knowledge was futile if I could not apply it to myself. I didn't want to burden you at the time, because of mother's illness . . . If it hadn't been for starting in a new field at the London I think . . . Anyway, I never wanted to see a woman again, except as a patient. But now . . . well, in a way it's rather frightening how one does get over things. Does it mean that no emotion can last?'

'You are more qualified to answer than I,' Ambrose replied, wiping a saucepan. 'But if I have learned anything from my sixty-five years on this planet, it is to be grateful for any mercies, and the passage of time can be one of the greatest.'

The next day they went for a drive to give Anne-Marie an idea of the Border countryside. After some time they found themselves passing through the village of Owlwick, which they noticed was built of reddish stone rather than the pencil-

38

grey of the cottages near Ambrose's home. A few minutes later he asked Peter to pause where a tree-lined avenue led across a field to a distant farmhouse.

'That's Owlwick Grange,' he said. 'It's the scene of one of the strangest supernatural happenings I have ever heard of.'

'Do tell us,' said Anne-Marie as the car moved forward again. 'I love your English ghost melodramas.'

'I got an inkling of the story when I was reading a Victorian writer named Theodore Hall and came across a tale about this place which seemed too dramatic to be true,' Ambrose said. 'It concerned the Russells – two Australian brothers and their sister – who took a lease on the house in 1874. One night the following summer Pamela Russell was awakened by the scratching of fingernails on her window. Whatever it was appeared to be unpicking the lead strips which held the small panes of glass together. It managed to get into the room where it attacked Pamela and bit her throat before her brothers arrived in answer to her screams. But the vampire escaped through the window and was last seen running down the drive in the direction of the Owlwick churchyard.

'The girl was so shocked by her experience her brothers took her to Switzerland for a long holiday. When they returned she was fully recovered, and was inclined to believe that she had been attacked by a large monkey which had probably escaped from some circus menagerie.

'Then, one night in March, 1876, she was aroused by the horribly familiar scratch of nails on glass. Her cries brought one brother to her room and the other, Edward, to the yard with a gun. By the light of the moon he saw what he later described as a "tall spindly fellow in a curious cloak" at his sister's window. The figure leapt away, and once more raced down the tree-lined avenue. Edward fired after it and it stumbled before continuing over the fields towards the churchyard.

'Realizing it was no ordinary prowler, the Russell brothers called in some neighbours and the local gamekeeper, and at dawn they began a search of the burial ground. One searcher noticed that a stone slab was out of place and when they investigated they found a "mummified" body in the space below. A great bonfire was lit and when the ancient corpse was taken to it they saw that there was a bullet hole in its thigh.'

'Bravo,' cried Anne-Marie. 'A very good story.'

'I was inclined to dismiss it as just that – a piece of fiction,' said Ambrose. 'But when I accidentally came across other references to it I got interested. When I came here I thought I'd take a look at the Grange out of curiosity. I went up that avenue and met the wife of the farmer who has it now, explaining that I was interested in the building. I did not mention the vampire as I did not want her to think I was a crank.

'The lady was very gracious, and when she had finished feeding her chickens she showed me round. But though the building was very old and full of historical interest – there's a priest-hole, for example – there appeared to be nothing about it to link it with Theodore Hall's account. I was just coming to the conclusion that the tale was a hoax when the lady pointed to a bricked-up window on the ground floor.

' "That was blocked up after the vampire got in and attacked Miss Russell," she said in a matter of fact way. And she went on to relate the story which is told locally exactly as I had first read it at the British Museum Reading Room.'

As he drove back towards the A69, Peter said: 'When I was doing psychology I got fascinated in trying to trace the origins of mythology in the human *moeurs*. It seemed to me that many legends were the result of folk memory. Take lycanthropy – that is *le loup garou*,' he explained to Anne-Marie. 'According to the legends a werewolf bite causes the victim to become one himself. With hydrophobia the infection is passed on by the bite of a rabid animal and the sufferer does begin to behave like a frenzied beast. He slavers, makes animal sounds and tries to bite those about him. It was easy for the superstitious to believe in werewolves once they had seen a man infected by rabies. Silver bullets and protective spells were poetic licence.'

'Then what about vampires?' asked Ambrose. 'Accounts of them are to be found in the ancient writings of Babylon and Assyria, but can you suggest what started them off? I agree that we are constantly learning there is a thread of truth in myths. Troy was just a legend until Heinrich Schliemann used Homer's poetry to locate its ruins. The Labyrinth of the Minotaur was a frightening fairy story until Sir Arthur Evans discovered the maze under the palace of Minos at Knossos.'

'I think I may have an example of a disorder which could have started the vampire cult,' mused Peter.

That night Ambrose was tired and went up to his bed early and for a while Peter and Anne-Marie sat in silence before the flickering wood fire. There seemed to be no need to talk. Suddenly she looked him in the face with her eyes mysterious in the warm glow.

'Peter, you can share my bed tonight if you wish.'

'You don't have to say that. . . .'

'I know. . . .'

He was quiet for a minute, seeking the right words.

'Anne-Marie . . . I don't know how to express this without sounding like some sort of weird prude . . . Somehow I'm afraid you are not ready, and I don't want to spoil anything which promises to be so good. . . .'

She laughed, partly with relief.

'You are very thoughtful. I think you have some idea why I left Paris for London. I want to be sure all that is behind me. But please promise you'll come running if I hear a scratching at my window.'

'If there's a scratching at your window it'll be me,' Peter joked. Both laughed and began to kiss tenderly, then passionately. They realized with some surprise this was the first time they had truly kissed. And with the increasing warmth of their embrace, their thoughts as to whether they were ready or not for a new phase in their relationship were forgotten in the tide of mounting emotional and sexual excitement.

Time became unimportant. They were only conscious of the easy fusion of their bodies, followed by wave after wave of intense pleasure until Anne-Marie gave a long shuddering sigh and Peter had the sensation of dropping away from the world into a void of warmth and darkness, the *petite mort* which no previous experience had given him.

Reality returned when Anne-Marie murmured in his ear: 'My love, I never believed in such an idea before, but we must have been designed for each other.'

Back at the London Hospital for Diseases of the Nervous System a nylon-smocked girl from the pathological laboratory carefully carried her tray into the Fleming Ward. She nodded to Sister and entered the narcoleptics' room where a cheerful Australian nurse kept a bored eye on the slumbering children.

'Dr Pilgrim wants blood samples from all of them,' the girl explained. 'He'll want the results when he comes back on Monday.'

She placed the tray on the locker by Britt's bed. Beneath the napkin there were over forty test-tubes held in wooden racks with their rounded bases resting safely on foam plastic. At the neck of each was an adhesive label in which was a ball-pointed name and number. These tubes, each three-quarters full of dark red fluid, represented the hospital's daily collection of blood samples.

Britt opened her eyes and smiled up at the girl prettily.

'Does she understand any English?'

The nurse shook her head.

'I wish I knew Swedish for "this won't hurt",' the girl muttered as she removed the cover from the tray, picked up a long-needled syringe and depressed the plunger. Britt's eyes narrowed at the sight of the rows of gleaming test-tubes.

'Mind if I shoot through to the loo for a minute?' the nurse asked, standing up stiffly and yawning. 'It's my chance while you're here because these kids mustn't be left alone.'

'That's okay,' replied the lab assistant as she tightened a tourniquet above the child's elbow to dilate the veins. The nurse left and with a kindly smile the girl prepared to ease the hypodermic needle into Britt's arm. But before the point pierced the skin, Britt wrenched herself back and with a strong upward sweep of her free arm struck the specimen tray. Test-tubes cascaded upwards in a fountain of flying glass. They smashed against walls and some even hit the ceiling, causing a shower of bloody droplets to rain on the Swedish girl's bed.

Alerted by the crash and the cries of the lab assistant, Sister ran in followed by an alarmed nurse. Glass fragments glittered on the floor while the blood of two score patients seemed to have spattered the whole room. But it was not the thought that she would have to take the samples again that was making the girl hysterical.

'Look, look!' she shrieked to Sister. 'Look what they're doing. . . .'

The commotion had aroused the children to full wakefulness and now they were jumping and crawling about the room in a frenzy, licking the venous blood as it dribbled down the bright walls.

Only Britt remained in bed with a look of composure on her beautiful face.

'*Blodet*,' she murmured. '*God blodet, god blodet.*'

5

In Copenhagen Holly Archer walked into the foyer of a sex theatre, paying her fee to a bored girl who sat knitting.

'This way,' said a small man in a dinner jacket. 'The live show will start soon. Meanwhile you can enjoy the blue movies.'

She was ushered into a long room with a small cinema screen at the far end. Rays of coloured light stabbed the cigarette smoke from an 8 mm projector to portray two masked but otherwise unclothed girls whipping a rather languid young man. Below the screen was an extra large mattress with a box of Kleenex at one side.

Holly settled herself beneath the projection window, and looked with curiosity at her fellow voyeurs. There were several young men sitting by themselves; a group of well-dressed businessmen, perhaps from Germany, and a middle-aged couple holding hands. ('American,' decided Holly, noting the man's tartan sports coat.)

There was a pause in the clicking of the projector and then a new epic about an *au pair* girl began.

A young man and woman took up seats in front of Holly, followed by a tall man in a black suit who sat down a seat away from her on the right. As the film reached its inevitable climax an English couple sat in the front row. ('Must try and get their reactions,' thought Holly. *'After what Ah've seen 'ere all Ah can say is that sex in 'Uddersfield is in its infancy....'*)

45

The little man from the foyer appeared and spoke in Danish then American: 'Folks, now the audience is complete, we have pleasure in giving you the best live sex in wonderful, wonderful Copenhagen. It's finger lickin' good.'

He stepped into the shadows and pop music vibrated from stereo amplifiers. A young girl stepped out of a curtained door near the mattress. With a slight, unexpected start Holly realized she was only about fifteen as, in a very matter of fact way, she began to unbutton her blouse. Unlike strippers Holly had once seen in Soho, the girl ignored the music and made no attempt to move to it. There was something strangely naïve about her; to Holly it was like watching a large child getting undressed for bed.

She shrugged off her blouse and, standing in a black bra, began to fumble with the waistband of her skirt. It seemed so artless, yet there was also something oddly impelling about it. The men in the audience had leaned forward, their eyes focused on her hands.

The skirt dropped to her ankles and she stepped out of the circle of material; twisting awkwardly she unfastened her bra. For a moment she stood with her hands dangling limply by her sides while the combined gaze of the audience caressed her immature breasts. Then she slipped out of her pants and squatted on the mattress. She put her arms behind her and leaned backwards like an acrobat, her head almost touching the rug as she arched her body. Holly was conscious of the hiss of indrawn breath round her. She might have been at a religious ceremony where a sacred relic was suddenly displayed for worship.

Music thudded through the room and slowly the girl resumed a standing attitude. She smiled at the audience for the first time, came forward and sat on the knee of a stranger in the front row. She guided his hand over her breasts and moved on to another. When she reached the American

46

couple she slid her hand over the man's thigh but his wife stood up and stalked to the exit. He followed sheepishly to muted laughter.

The naked girl raised her shoulders, and went on to the next customer. After she had finished her round, she slipped into a kimono, collected her scattered garments from the mattress and walked out. At the same time the lights, which had been dimmed during the performance, came up and several girls walked in with glasses and bottles of Tuborg lager for general refreshment. With a mental shrug Holly thought: So that's what it's all about!

The next act was a conventional striptease, followed by a lesbian exhibition in which two girls wrestled, embraced and caressed each other with purrs of pleasure and a growing un-awareness – perhaps cleverly assumed – of the audience. To Holly's surprise this seemed to have an electrifying effect on the males in the audience who stared with rapt expressions as the couple squirmed and kissed. She noticed the pair in front of her had their arms round each other's shoulders and were huddling together like excited children. God knew what effect it was having on them!

She glanced sideways at the man on her right. Silhouetted against the glow of a spotlight she saw a fine profile with hair curling over the forehead. He seemed to be the only one not rapt over the lesbians' routine. He looked at her with what seemed to Holly a slightly cynical smile.

Next came the girl who had taken the entrance money in the foyer. She held a battery-powered vibro machine which, amidst laughter, she began to use on the nearest man.

'Here we believe in audience participation,' she joked as she deftly wielded the device. 'Would any ladies here like to try it?' Holly found herself blushing hotly as she shook her head.

So the show continued. The room filled with the tang of

sweat and sexuality, and a static electricity of excitement emanated by the men – no, Holly had to admit – by the women, too. She felt she was the only one not turned on by the performances. She was still a little sickened by the first act – that young girl should be doing homework and going to bed with a hot drink rather than spreading her thighs for anonymous adults.

Then Holly noticed the stranger on her right seemed equally aloof. She could not see him clearly but she sensed it would take a lot more than this mattress-tumbling to arouse him.

The finale was announced and the young performer Holly had been thinking about walked out in her silk kimono. Another figure appeared, the MC who had changed his evening dress for a white towelling dressing gown. Only one spotlight illuminated the two pale figures standing ceremoniously opposite each other.

Holly thought: They're like Japanese *judoka*.

Unselfconsciously they slipped off their robes and – with an oddly touching gesture – kissed each other gently on the lips. Music pulsed, heavy and savage with electronic distortion. 'Go! Go! Go!' cried a singer before he was drowned under a thundering wave of percussion.

Almost reluctantly the performers relinquished their chaste embrace. This time it was Holly who sucked in her breath as she watched the male performer become aroused by caresses of his partner. They were not the caresses of lovers. The couple appeared to be fighting each other, trying to tear each other's body with their hands. Yet they moved with a certain grace, perhaps born of long practice.

First one then the other sank to the mattress beneath the onslaught of their partner. Like dancers they assumed position after position, sometimes grotesquely and sometimes with an erotic dignity.

48

As the music surged towards a crescendo, a strong hand gripped Holly's but she was now so intent on what was happening she hardly noticed and was only aware the stranger had moved beside her.

In the merciless spotlight the girl closed her eyes and opened her mouth to emit a husky wail as the man clasped her to him and their bodies began to tremble in unison. Holly could hear the whistling of their breath above the booming beat background. She felt like crying out with their cries. Everything had lost importance except those writhing figures and the mysterious hand which gripped hers so tight, sending electric impulses up her arm.

Both performers were drenched in sweat. Like silver rain it glistened on their bodies as they parted from each other only to reunite in some new and more abandoned pose.

Tears streamed down Holly's face and her heart raced as a wave of hysteria rose to engulf her. The couple were on their feet again. Seconds later the girl tore herself away from her partner, leaving him forlorn yet proving the performance had been genuine.

Holly sank back, her free hand across her eyes.

'You must come with me,' said the stranger. 'This is nothing to what is possible.' Turning her head, she saw that his expression was strained. His eyes were still focused on the performers. Following his gaze to where the girl was helping her exhausted partner into his robe, Holly saw a thin line of blood creeping like a worm down the man's chest. The result of an erotic scratch, the sight of it made her almost lightheaded.

She was hardly aware of being led out of the musky theatre to a long black Mercedes with ticking engine at the kerb. She was helped into the fur-upholstered back seat.

A dark figure, with long hair falling from under a rakish chauffeur's cap, lounged behind the wheel. She addressed the

49

stranger as 'Stromberg', and spoke some words in oddly-accented French before the big car accelerated into the cold night.

Anne-Marie, in a white raincoat with epaulettes and a matching white beret, walked into the Black Sheep coffee bar which was usually deserted at this early evening hour. Peter Pilgrim was hunched in a corner seat, and she could tell by the bleak smile he gave her that he was very worried. He tried to hide it when he said: 'Hello, darling. You look very stylish in that outfit. I hope you're not too knocked out after such a packed weekend.'

She ordered a lemon tea and said: 'It was a lovely weekend, but the grapevine says you came back to problems.'

'It doesn't lie,' he answered. 'While we were away my patients went berserk. Britt upset a tray of blood samples and they licked it like dogs in a slaughterhouse. There's no explanation other than Britt. She attacked that wretched orderly, and the other children . . . it's starting to give me a rather wild idea.'

The French girl sipped her tea.

'I know what you're going to say. I, too, remember what your father told us about Owlwick Grange.'

'What happened there was put down to a vampire,' Peter said.

'And you can hardly write in your report there's an outbreak of vampirism in the London. Sir Henry would have you struck off.'

'I think I'm on to something so rare that in the past, whenever it happened, it was startling enough to give rise to legends. It's happened before. In mediaeval Europe there was the Dancing Madness when whole villages jigged in the streets for days. Then Satan was blamed. Now we know

50

those villagers were the victims of ergot poisoning which they got through bread made from fungus-infected rye.'

Anne-Marie put her hand on his. '*Pauvre chéri*, I know it is very worrying for you, but in the end it could make your reputation.'

'If only that cow of a nurse hadn't dozed off when Britt interfered with the others,' he said, scowling at his empty cup. 'Matron is up in arms in case the parents lodge complaints. Even though I'd asked for full surveillance after the orderly business, I'm still responsible. They'll say I should have had her isolated.'

'It's not the first time a patient has got violent at the London,' said Anne-Marie consolingly.

'My father's coming down to stay with my aunt in Chiswick. I've written asking him to dig up everything he can on the vampire myth just in case there could be a connection. Now let's forget it for a while. I've got the car round the corner and we could go to Regent's Park and take a walk.'

A few minutes later they left the Citroën by the park entrance. A drizzle fell, so fine it glistened on Anne-Marie's hair like yellow diamonds in the pale glow of the lamps lining the inner circle. She turned up her collar and they walked hand in hand, enjoying the odour of damp earth and the mysterious shadows of trees silhouetted against the orange aureole of the city.

'You know I return to France soon,' Anne-Marie said.

'That's the other thing that's bothering me,' said Peter. 'I don't want you marrying some handsome young French surgeon.'

'I won't be marrying,' she said with an ironical laugh. 'Listen, Peter-Pierre, before I get work in Paris I'm going for a holiday at a house belonging to an old family friend. It has a lovely name – *La Maison des Papillons* – and it's on the edge of the Camargue. Spend a fortnight there with me.'

'I wish I could, but how can I leave my patients at this critical stage?'

'I know,' she admitted reluctantly. 'But you would love the Camargue. Every year Gypsies come from all over Europe to worship their saint at Saintes Maries de la Mer. It is both a carnival and religious festival – there is dancing and bull-fighting and processions. It's what you need. You look so . . . so serious these days.'

For a while they strolled in silence. In the distance they could hear a lion roar in the zoo. It was a powerful and primitive sound and a reminder that while civilization might give the illusion of comfort and security, primitive forces were still abroad like barbarians prowling the frontiers of Rome. Peter felt Anne-Marie shiver against him.

'A goose must have walked over my grave,' she said.

6

While Peter and Anne-Marie were walking in the fine drizzle, the ward orderly Lionel Tedworth arrived at a decaying Georgian house in a decaying street less than a quarter of a mile east of the park. Having checked its number against a scrap of smudged newsprint, he rang the bell and waited. A man in a white sweater, whose middle age was betrayed only by his curling silver hair, opened the door.

'Good evening. I'm Mr Tedworth. I phoned earlier on.'

'Welcome,' said the man in the sweater. 'I'm counsellor for tonight's session. Call me Sam. Hang your coat in the hall, and I'll take the donation now.'

Lionel handed him a couple of pounds and was ushered into a bare room. The only furnishings were cushions strewn about a worn carpet which smelled faintly of cats. A dozen people – nearly all younger than himself, Lionel noted with trepidation – were lotus-positioned on these. Some showed their tension by smoking rapidly.

Sam took the centre of the floor. 'Our group is complete now. Er, Lionel, I suggest you take off your shoes and get yourself a cushion. Before we begin I would like to welcome those of you who haven't been to the Bloomsbury Human Communication Centre before.'

From the circle of cushions the small audience gazed hopefully at Sam. There was something indefinably lost and languid about most of the group. This disappointed Lionel; perhaps he had expected too much from these contact sessions he had read about. Run by several progressive groups, they competed to help the lonely gain confidence and establish therapeutic relationships with their fellows.

This is what Lionel felt he needed. Outside hospital life he had no contact with the world, and he realized this because of a feeling that something mysterious had happened to his personality after Britt's attack. He experienced a desperate compulsion to join the mainstream of humanity, but were these nervous strangers the support he needed?

'. . . for the sake of newcomers to our drop-in session I'd better explain a little of what we do here,' Sam was saying. 'Freedom is the key word. Feel free to express yourselves however you like. Don't let old-fashioned bourgeois taboos hold you back. If you want to swear or use so-called dirty words, use them at the top of your voice. Nobody is going to be shocked or, if they are, it's a bloody good thing for them. While you can be as free as you like, no one has the right to interfere with the freedom of others, so we draw the line at violence.

'You'll see the form the session takes as we go along, and I'll explain the philosophy behind it afterwards. Remember, I'm not a director but a catalyst, I'm merely here to get things moving – you have to liberate yourselves. And now, on your feet, friends, and we'll start with exercises.'

Lionel stood up with embarrassment and had the consolation of sensing some of the others were embarrassed too, though several veterans looked forward with shining-eyed expectation to the good time that was to come.

Sam said with authority: 'I want you to walk about with your eyes closed and with your arms folded, and just bump into each other.'

Lionel understood that basic contact between human beings came through physical touch, but he couldn't imagine it assuaging the strange longings which had recently begun to torment his subconscious.

A blind, aimless walk began again. A youth nudged Lionel and shouted: 'Piss off, you sodding bastard!'

Lionel felt some resentment at this rudeness, but could not find it in himself to reply in similar terms. The words of abuse cleared the way for everyone else and within seconds the room rang with insults and curses.

'Splendid!' enthused Sam.

Next the group was encouraged to jump up and down with their eyes still closed, breathing deep and shouting. Lionel was surprised to hear some of the words, particularly from a pale but buxom young woman who bounced up and down like a mechanical toy beside him. A tang of sweat filled the room as the group continued to leap and let their inhibitions crumble.

'That was a good start,' Sam declared. 'Now I'm going to ask each one of you in turn who you are and why you're here. You first,' and he pointed to a bearded young man.

'I'm William Head,' he said with difficulty. Lionel saw his eyes were dangerously moist. 'I've . . . I've . . . I've come because I have great . . . great difficulty . . . in getting along with . . . people. People . . . frighten me.'

A thin-faced, smartly dressed young man gave his name quickly, and added: 'I'm frightened, too.'

When it came to Lionel's turn, he did not know what to say. Mentally he asked himself: 'Why *am* I here?' Something held him back from admitting the truth, so, with lowered head, he mumbled: 'Like the others, I'm scared.' He realized that, after all, he had perhaps spoken the truth.

As the evening passed with activities and discussion to break down inhibitions, tension mounted which was heightened by periodic personal dramas. A girl, who announced she hated her mother, was invited to sit cross-legged before a cushion.

'You must imagine that the cushion is your mother, and you've got to tell her how you loathe her,' Sam said.

'But I can't,' the girl protested. 'She only died three months ago.'

'All the more reason,' Sam said. 'Come on, Sally, lay the ghost!'

Sally gave the cushion a couple of weak blows, whispering: 'I hate you, Mummy. I hate you, Mummy.' As the clamour of encouragement increased round her, she began to beat more fiercely, raising a cloud of dust with her clenched fists.

'I hate you, Mummy! I hate you, Mummy!' she shouted. Tears gave way to laughter as she finally fell back exhausted.

'Now for something more formal,' Sam announced. 'Each find a partner.'

Lionel found himself opposite Sylvia, a girl whose long black hair hung untidily over a man's red sports shirt.

'Okay?' he asked hesitantly.

She nodded.

'One of you must say: "Who are you?" ' Sam instructed. 'And the other must answer and then the first one will say: "Thank you", and then immediately ask again: "Who are you?" This goes on for five minutes, and then you reverse roles.'

'You go first,' Sylvia muttered.

'All right,' said Lionel. 'Who are you?'

'I'm Sylvia,' she replied and stopped.

'Thank you, Sylvia,' said Lionel. 'Who are you?'

'I'm Sylvia, and I live alone in a bedsit.'

'Thank you,' said Lionel. 'Who are you?'

'I'm Sylvia, and I'm a student but I can't communicate with the others who go to my classes.'

'Thank you. Who are you?'

'I'm Sylvia, and I'm 23, and I don't trust men and I hated my father and I wish I didn't bite my fingernails.'

'Thank you. Who are you?'

'I'm Sylvia,' she whispered sorrowfully. 'And I don't seem to get my relationships right. I like people – I mean, I'd like to have friends and all that. I'd like to love someone, but each time this happens they want things from me I cannot give.' She began to get desperate.

'I'm Sylvia,' she stated, normal again. 'And I think the whole world needs putting right. I hate the Government, and I'm on the side of the blacks and I'm for Irish Civil Rights and the *tupamaros*, and I think our consumer society is rotten through and through and I'm for revolt.'

'Thank you. Who are you?'

And so the game went on, and Lionel realized the simple 'Thank you – who are you?' formula probably brought more to the surface in a few minutes than hours on a psychiatrist's couch. When it was Sylvia's turn to lead, Lionel played his hand skilfully.

'I'm Lionel Tedworth,' he told her. 'And I agree society is rotten. I believe we should all do something positive about it, make our own contribution no matter how small. That is why I work with sick people. . . .' He stopped, pretending embarrassment at this admission.

'Thank you,' she said, impressed. 'Who are you?'

'I'm Lionel Tedworth. Like you I don't seem to be able to make deep relationships. I mean, genuine ones, not those based on . . .' Here he faltered and Sylvia nodded sympathetically.

'Thank you, Lionel. Who are you?'

'I'm Lionel Tedworth, and I'd very much like to see you after this session for coffee.'

'Thank you,' she said and smiled at him suddenly, and

equally suddenly he felt the evening was going to be a success after all.

They arrived at her room above an old shop in Chalk Farm at midnight. Lionel tiptoed on the creaking stairs but she said: 'Don't worry about noise. The couple opposite my room are away, and old Mr Hertz upstairs is so deaf he can't hear anything. I can always play my record player as loud as I like.'

She unlocked an apple-green door on the first landing and took Lionel into a large room with a high, old-fashioned ceiling. In one corner was a curtained sink, in another was a legless bed with a pile of books by it. In the centre a record player rested on a coffee table, while an old kitchen table covered with books and papers stood beneath the high sash window. The wallpaper was mercifully faded.

Lionel saw that Sylvia had tried to brighten the room with posters, a blow-up of a romantic-looking guerilla leader, another of a Chinese girl's torso, and a coloured print of the earth photographed from an Apollo rocket.

'Coffee?'

'Please,' said Lionel from the edge of her bed.

'I thought Sam was brilliant tonight,' Sylvia said, spooning coffee granules into a pair of mugs while an electric kettle steamed on her work table. 'You didn't join in much,' she added accusingly.

'No, but I did try.'

She handed him a hot mug and sat at the far end of the bed.

'What's your real hang-up, Lionel?'

'I don't really know,' he confessed. 'Lately I have had feelings of doom – that, without me understanding it, something dreadful has been happening to me.'

'I know what you mean. I've had a feeling of dread since I

58

was a little girl. I think it's a dread of society — I mean, society as it is now, corrupted by money. I was thinking of throwing up college and working on a kibbutz, but now I think I'll become a communication counsellor like Sam. He was telling me of a course which makes you a qualified counsellor in three months. What do you do at the hospital? You're not a doctor, are you? I hope not. Doctors are sick. They won't even recognize acupuncture....'

'I'm a sort of . . .' Lionel's mind tried to think of what he could be. 'Massage is my line,' he said. 'Yes, I specialize in massage.'

His truthful conscience, which had been the pride of his mother, reflected that this was hardly a falsehood. He rubbed about twenty pairs of buttocks twice daily with liquid soap and spirit to prevent bed sores.

'You must get inspiration, touching so many people. I want to touch people all the time, but unfortunately they take it the wrong way. They see something sexual in it.'

'I suppose they do,' Lionel mused. 'People can be so unenlightened.'

'Right,' she said. 'Of course, I'm all for sexual freedom. One day I'd like to go in for group marriage, but I think it's important a relationship is built on something more than reaction between people's glands. I mean, I've got a mind.'

'Of course,' Lionel agreed automatically, his thoughts occupied with a strange hunger which made his hands tremble as he held the coffee mug.

'I mean, a relationship should be beautiful and happy and fun and not based on screwing. But it seems all the men I meet are only interested in bed. Like my father. Sometimes I think all men are the same. They want to use women the way my father used my Mum.'

'Perhaps not all.'

'Perhaps not. I think I could trust you, Lionel,' she told

59

him, looking into his plump face. 'You're sort of older and more mature. I mean, if I didn't trust you I wouldn't let you come into my room tonight, would I? I must tell you that I think sex is something holy, and one can't have something holy with just anyone, can one?'

'I don't know,' he answered. He had hardly been listening to her earnest words. His mind had been struggling to control the frightful images which drifted like phantasmagoria from his troubled subconscious.

'Are you all right?' the girl asked. 'You look a bit . . .'

'I think I'm all right, but perhaps I'd better go.'

'Oh, don't leave yet, Lionel. If you are upset about something you can tell me.'

He was not sure how it happened, but before he could get to his feet the girl was close beside him, her arms round his neck, and under her weight both fell back across the bed. With a clumsy movement she switched off the standard lamp above them. Now there was only the glow of a small reading lamp on the table, and by it Lionel watched her bend over him, her lank hair tickling his face as she came closer. Air hissed softly through her teeth. Her lips pressed painfully against his, her tongue seeking entrance to his mouth. For a moment he could hardly believe what was happening, then he abandoned himself to the fearful excitement which swept over him as side by side they panted with the force of their fantasies.

'Oh love, oh love,' Sylvia moaned, her hands dancing over his chest and along his thighs. 'Let me take this shirt off. I want you to hold me.'

For a moment she sat up, tugging the maroon acrilan shirt over her head. She was without a bra, and as Lionel saw her ivory skin the excitement tightened within him like some terrible spring. Experimentally he ran his fingertips down

60

her back. With a whimper she was beside him again.

'You have magic fingers. No wonder you are a healer. Love me with your hands.' Sylvia rolled on to her stomach, her face buried in the pillow while Lionel knelt on the bed beside her, his trembling hands sliding up and down her back.

'Oh yes, oh yes,' she cried as his fingers made furrows of pleasure along her flesh. From then on their words became mere noises as they rolled and grappled. Soon they were naked, and the girl knelt on the bed, her head down, her hair falling to the blanket.

'From the back,' she commanded.

Lionel saw the vertebrae taut under the smooth skin. His hands continued to run over the firm flesh. Leaning forward, he reached beneath her chest and kneaded the soft breasts which swung free with her shivering rapture.

With his left hand again massaging her spine in time to the rhythm of their bodies, he frantically reached for his wallet with his right. He pulled it from the hip pocket of his trousers and managed to open it. In the stamp pocket he felt something sharp and, with a grunt of satisfaction, withdrew a scalpel blade. Until now it had been a pencil sharpener.

Holding it firmly between his finger and thumb, he drew the micro-sharpened point gently across the shoulders of the girl writhing against him. The skin parted neatly at the touch of the steel. It was as easy as pulling a zipper, and by the time the blade had reached the end of the stroke blood was beading where the incision began. Sylvia seemed unaware of what was happening, her body too excited by the phrenetic stimulation of the stranger.

While Lionel's body continued to play the role of the frenzied lover, his detached mind looked down on the ragged line of blood with delight never experienced before. Again the narrow blade crossed the sweat-sheened skin, again so deftly that blood welled without Sylvia realizing what was happening.

With a harsh cry she collapsed across the bed and Lionel followed, his mouth greedily following the long scalpel cuts. The salt taste actually made him shout.

'Ah, Lionel, I'm so glad, I'm so glad,' murmured Sylvia Then she demanded: 'What have you done? My back, it's warm and wet . . . surely . . .'

She squirmed from beneath him, looked at his face, gave a shuddering cry and fainted. When Lionel reeled to the sink, he saw why. A spotted mirror reflected features dyed by the quenching of an unnatural thirst.

He wiped himself with a dishcloth, mechanically collected his mangled clothing and dressed. With chilling certainty he knew now exactly what he must do. He gave a professional glance at the body on the smeared bed, threw an old eiderdown over it and walked into the haunted night.

7

The night was wet and cold in Romilly Street as Peter led his father into La Capannina, but the welcome from the waiters to the narrow restaurant made them feel they had entered the tropics after an arctic winter. The proprietor, Gianni, seated them at a corner table and asked: 'Is the young French lady coming tonight, doctor?'

'She'll be along later,' Peter replied, explaining to Ambrose that Anne-Marie was delayed at the hospital. He turned to Gianni. 'Do you mind if we wait with our drinks until she arrives?'

'Of course not, signor. Take your time, but may I say the *osso buco alla Milanese* is very good tonight.'

Ambrose looked round the room with approval. It was already more than half full, and the clamour of animated conversation was rising. He recognized a television actress and began to feel that after his lonely life in Northumberland he was back at the hub of things.

'Before the charming Anne-Marie arrives I'll give you these notes I made on vampirism at the British Museum Reading Room,' he said to his son, passing over an exercise book filled with his neat writing. 'It's all I could glean at short notice.'

'It looks as though you worked hard,' Peter said, turning the pages and noting the headings. 'I'm very grateful.'

'I had my reward,' smiled Ambrose. 'I came across a fasci-nating case, so interesting that I feel there is a book to be

63

written about it. But may I ask why you – a doctor in the 1970s – should be interested in such an odd and ancient subject. I should have thought you men of science would have dismissed Dracula and his kind as old wives' nonsense.'

'There's something so strange happening with my special patients that I'm leaving no stone unturned to try and find some clue to it. Remember I said that lycanthropy legends were probably born as a result of people suffering with hydrophobia. Now I'm looking to legends for some hint of behaviour which at the moment baffles me. Perhaps it is a crazy line of research, but this appetite for blood . . .' And he went on to explain the situation in Fleming Ward.

By the time they had finished they were on their second drink. Ambrose shook his silvery mane.

'I'm afraid my gleanings are not likely to help you much,' he admitted. 'Vampires in a super modern hospital like yours seem too far-fetched. While I thrive on old legends, I must admit I agree with you about their non-supernatural origins. In the case of this particular myth it probably began as an explanation from the activities of sufferers from necrophilia. In which case I'm afraid there is nothing in the belief to help you.'

From the waiters came the sound of enthusiastic greetings and Peter looked up to see Anne-Marie, the target of many eyes in a white velvet dress, walk into the restaurant.

'Hello, darling,' she said as Peter rose and gave her a kiss of welcome. 'Hello, dear friend,' she said to Ambrose. 'A whisky and Coke,' she added to Gianni.

'How revolting,' exclaimed Ambrose in mock horror.

The French girl smiled and raised her shoulders in an exaggerated Continental gesture.

'Blame Les Beatles. They made it the rage of Paris when I was small, and so to me it appeared to be a really trendy drink. Now I am grown up it still has some sort of associa-

64

tion from those far-off days when I used to save my few francs each week to buy their singles.'

They bent their heads over the menus, chuckling over such fractured English as 'nuck of veal served with jellow nice'. After their orders had been taken, Anne-Marie said: 'Don't let me interrupt you. I understand Peter is trying to get your help in solving his narcoleptic problem. That story you told us about Owlwick Grange gave him the idea.'

'He has all my notes,' said Ambrose, 'so there's no point in detailing the horrors of the nastiest creatures in folklore.'

'You said there was one case that particularly interested you,' said Peter.

'Ah, yes. That is because it is historically accurate.'

'You must tell us,' said Anne-Marie as her *sogliola di Dover* was placed before her.

Ambrose sipped his wine and then brought out a note-book.

'Let me read you this translation from Michael Wagener's *Beitrage zur philosopischen Anthropologie*, which was published in Vienna in 1796,' he said. ' "Elizabeth (name suppressed, family still living) was wont to dress well to please her husband, and she spent half a day over her toilet. On one occasion, a lady's maid saw something wrong in her head-dress, and as a recompense for observing it, received such a severe box on the ears that the blood gushed from her nose, and spurted on to her mistress's face. When the blood drops were washed off her face, her skin appeared much more beautiful – whiter and much more transparent on the spots where the blood had been.

' "Elizabeth formed the resolution to bathe her face and her whole body in human blood so as to enhance her beauty. Two old women and a certain Fitzko assisted her in her undertaking. This monster used to kill the luckless victim, and the old women caught the blood, in which Elizabeth

65

was wont to bathe at the hour of four in the morning. After the bath she appeared more beautiful than before.

' "She continued this habit after the death of her husband (1604) in the hopes of gaining new suitors. The unhappy girls who were lured to the castle, under the plea that they were to be taken into service there, were locked up in a cellar. Here they were beaten till their bodies were swollen. Elizabeth not infrequently tortured the victims herself; often she changed their clothes which dripped with blood, and then renewed her cruelties. The swollen bodies were then cut with razors.

' "Occasionally she had the girls burned, and then cut up, but the great majority were beaten to death. At last her cruelty became so great that she would stick needles into those who sat with her in a carriage, especially if they were of her own sex. One of her servant girls she stripped naked, smeared her with honey, and so drove her out of the house. . . ." '

'Why do that?' interrupted Anne-Marie.

'To attract the forest insects to torment her, I suppose,' explained Ambrose. 'Anyway, to continue: "When she was ill, and could not indulge her cruelty, she bit a person who came near her sick-bed as though she were a wild beast.

' "She caused, in all, the death of six hundred and fifty girls, some in Tscheita, on the neutral ground, where she had a cellar constructed for the purpose; others in different localities, for murder and bloodshed became with her a necessity.

' "When at last the parents of the lost children could no longer be cajoled, the castle was seized, and the traces of the murders were discovered. Her accomplices were executed, and she was imprisoned for life." '

'What a horrible story,' exclaimed Anne-Marie. 'It is hard to believe a human being could be capable of such things.'

'Yes,' agreed Ambrose. 'She makes Gilles de Retz – the

original Bluebeard – look a mere amateur, yet he got all the publicity. Because of her aristocratic connections Elizabeth was never actually brought to trial and the details of her crimes were suppressed as much as possible. Wagener, writing nearly a century later, was afraid to mention her illustrious family name. However, truth will out, and if you look in *Chambers Biographical Dictionary*, you can find the following entry, and again I quote:

' "Bathori, Elizabeth, niece of Stephan, King of Poland, and wife of the Hungarian Count Nádasdy, was discovered in 1610 to have murdered six hundred and fifty young girls, that she might renew her own youth by bathing in their warm blood, but she was shut up for life in her fortress at Csej." '

The dessert came and Peter ordered Zambucca on the rocks. He recommended this house speciality to Anne-Marie, while Ambrose settled for a cognac.

'What happened to the vampire lady in the end?' asked Anne-Marie.

'She was walled up in a small room within her castle,' said Ambrose, 'with only a small space left for food to be passed to her. Four gibbets were erected on the ramparts to show that justice had been done unofficially.'

'Why unofficially?' asked Peter.

'Count Pal Nádasdy, the eldest son of Elizabeth (she had four children), wrote to the Lord Palatine in an endeavour to save his mother from punishment, and this saved her from the headsman's axe. Her accomplices were executed in ways that I will not describe while Anne-Marie is having her crème caramel.

'But, deprived of her supply of blood, Elizabeth did not survive long. A contemporary historian called Krapinai wrote of her, "Elizabeth Bathori, widow of Count Ferencz Nádasdy, His Majesty's Chief Master of Horse, who was notorious for her murders, died imprisoned at Csejthe castle on August 14, 1614, suddenly and without crucifix and without light." '

Ambrose put away his notebook.

'I'm afraid I got rather carried away by the Countess,' he said. 'I've got a newspaper cutting I found which might be of interest to you, Peter, but don't bother with it now.'

'Thanks for the research, Dad,' Peter said. 'I was hoping that something would emerge out of the superstition. It's such an old and universal myth and yet, when I come up against it in one of the world's best equipped hospitals, I find I'm utterly lost.'

Ambrose swirled his brandy round in the balloon glass thoughtfully and said: 'We're in a strange patch of human history. In this last century we have become drunk with power – and by power I mean energy. Until the oil crisis, each member of the world's population on average had at his disposal the equivalent of power supplied by twelve human slaves. In the United States the ratio has been a hundred slave-power to each citizen. Each time a jet crosses the Atlantic it burns up a swimming-pool of irreplaceable fuel and ten tons of oxygen . . . we have spent our resources with the abandon of drunken sailors in a brothel. . . .'

'That's a good literary phrase,' Anne-Marie chuckled.

'We have the illusion that nature has few secrets left because men have driven on the moon and, in less than a lifetime, we have replaced the crystal set with colour television. Now our energy resources are getting low, our lights are just beginning to dim, and who knows what will come creeping back from the shadows? Who knows what old taints will return to our blood . . . ?'

The Capannina guests looked up startled as Peter's fist suddenly crashed down on the table.

'Good God!' he breathed as the milky Zambucca from

68

his overturned glass soaked into the tablecloth. 'Why didn't I think of it before? Infected blood! What a blind idiot I've been. Infected blood!'

The London Hospital for Diseases of the Nervous System loomed vast against the mauve evening sky as Peter Pilgrim emerged from a narrow alley into Trinity Square. Already the old gas lamps – converted to take electric bulbs – were casting yellow haloes. Passing a statue of a long-deceased general on a charger, he glanced at the parallels of bright windows which marked the wards. Like all doctors he was familiar with human suffering, yet the quintessence of pain concentrated in the great brick edifice struck him morbidly.

Inside he took the lift up to Fleming Ward.

'How are my sleepers today?' he asked Sister.

'No changes. Jeremy has been restless. He's awake now.' She smiled sympathetically at the young doctor, which depressed him further, knowing it was because he was having no success with his patients.

He walked into the sub-ward and to a corner bed where a twelve-year-old boy gazed dreamily at the ceiling.

'Jeremy, how are you this evening?' he said, sitting on the bed, to Sister's private disapproval.

'All right,' the boy answered. 'Have you found out what's wrong with me yet?'

'We know that. You sleep too much.'

'Will I get better?'

'I hope so. That's why you're here, for us to make you well.'

Jeremy mused for a moment. 'I wonder what happens while I'm asleep; perhaps I'm awake somewhere else and when I go to sleep there I wake up here.'

'That's an interesting thought. The Australian Aborigines believe there is a Dream Time. Everything comes from the

Dream Time; not only people but kangaroos and plants and stones. When people go to sleep they go to the Dream Time. The Aborigines say the Dream Time is the real life and we're on a sort of holiday from it while we're on earth.'

'I like that,' said the child. 'Since I've been in hospital I must go to the Dream Time a lot and . . .' His voice trailed off and his eyelids closed. Once more he was in the unnatural slumber of narcolepsy.

The doctor straightened up and glanced at his watch. 'I'll look in later, Sister,' he said. 'I've got to go to Sir Henry's bun-fight now.'

He was the last to arrive in the common-room where Sir Henry Beresford had arranged a cocktail party to welcome Dr Axel Stromberg, the distinguished neurologist from Sweden who had come to the London to study a newly-introduced surgical technique. The party was a victory celebration for Sir Henry, underlining the fact that a consultant of Stromberg's standing considered he had something to learn from him.

Sir Henry Beresford was one of the two chief neuro-surgeons at the London; the other was Mr Robert Harvey. Each had his own 'school' of juniors, and it amused Peter Pilgrim to note the way the young men aped the manner-isms of their mentors.

The Beresford faction were given to flamboyant gestures, a supercilious attitude to the nursing staff and a complete disregard for the notion a patient might have a personality.

While Sir Henry had his black Rolls Royce whisk him to his Surrey estate each evening, Mr Robert Harvey mod-estly drove a grimy Cortina to a self-effacing house in a North London suburb. Sir Henry came from a distinguished line of medical men who on more than one occasion had taken a royal pulse; Mr Robert Harvey was a miner's son.

On the operating table Sir Henry performed with histrionics as well as great skill, amusing his fellow doctors with a flow of cultured anecdote and reducing theatre sisters to near hysteria at the slightest hesitation in following his crisp commands. Mr Robert Harvey approached his patients nervously, like a village clockmaker suddenly called upon to take a Piaget watch apart. Yet once the first incision was made he operated with quiet precision, speaking softly and kindly to the staff about him. His 'school' was equally humble and quiet-spoken.

As Peter Pilgrim took a glass of sherry he saw Sir Henry was standing possessively beside Dr Stromberg, a tall, equally elegant figure with glossy black hair curling over his forehead. His face was long with prominent cheekbones and a narrow nose such as once characterized certain elite families in central Europe. His skin was pale, with a bluish shadow on the finely shaved jowls. In contrast his dark red lips were full and had a downward curve. His deep brown eyes expressed lively intelligence.

'So that's old Beresford's latest catch,' said Tudor Owens. 'He's got a hell of a record, boy-o. As a kid he was in a DP camp, then a Swedish orphanage. Now he's got his own clinic financed by his own foundation.'

'Ah, Pilgrim,' Sir Henry interrupted. 'Dr Stromberg was particularly anxious to meet you after I told him of your research project.'

Peter shook hands with the tall man and found that despite his long, fragile-looking fingers he had, like many surgeons, tendons of steel.

'Dr Pilgrim, I am pleased to meet you,' he said in carefully modulated English. 'Already I have heard of your work with narcoleptics. This interests me very much because I have some such cases in my clinic. With them I have not progressed as I would have wished.'

'Neither have I,' Peter admitted. 'So far I have just eliminated some theoretical angles. In the past too much emphasis has been placed on the hyperthalamus. . . .'

'Ah, I am very interested to hear you say that. I have read with great interest your report in which you hypothesize the effect of blood factors on nervous centres. Perhaps tomorrow I could see your patients.'

Sir Henry was delighted that Dr Stromberg continued to talk for a long time to Dr Pilgrim – it kept him away from Mr Robert Harvey.

8

A tap at the door.

In her small room Mrs Kiss struggled out of her chair to get into a position to use her aluminium walking frame.

The tap was repeated.

'I am coming,' she called. 'Ai, ai. I come as fast as I can.' Her hands gripped the top of the frame. The upper part of her broad peasant body was still strong, only her legs had betrayed her. Foot by excruciating foot she moved towards the brown peeling door. Behind her ribs her heart fluttered like a trapped bird. Who could be calling on her? The welfare visitor was not due for another couple of hours. Could it be a postman? Would he go away before she could reach the door?

'Wait, wait, I come,' she shouted.

From behind the door came a muffled voice, deep with a slight foreign intonation (but not to Mrs Kiss whose English was deeply accented): 'Take your time. I shall wait.'

She achieved the door, turned the key and peered through the space permitted by the safety chain. The gloom of the landing baffled her eyes after the glare of her unshaded bulb which burned night and day, but she was aware of a tall figure in a black Continental raincoat. His face was a blur of white with two dark holes where the eyes ought to be. In panic she began to push the door against his foot.

'Are you Mrs Kiss – Elizabeth Kiss – who came to this country about twenty years ago?'

She paused, then asked: 'Are you from the Embassy?'

'I beg your pardon?'

'Ai, you do not understand.'

Like other East European refugees in Notting Hill Gate, Mrs Kiss lived in fear of the sinister 'men from the Embassy'. Mysterious officials in sunglasses, they visited émigrés to remind them that although they had escaped from their homelands, the People's Governments of those homelands had not forgotten them, nor forgiven.

'I am not from any embassy,' reassured the stranger. 'I am a lawyer. I am looking for a Mrs Kiss who once resided in the Csejthe district in north Hungary.'

'A lawyer, you say,' she muttered as she slipped the safety chain. 'You had better come in.' Painfully she moved to one side and the tall man entered.

'Sit please,' and she gestured to the chair used by the welfare visitor. Her mind was whirling and as she returned to her seat her hands trembled on the frame. In the light of the room she saw the stranger's eyes had appeared odd because he wore green-tinted glasses.

'It was because of the glasses I thought you were from the Embassy,' she explained with a nervous laugh as she surveyed the stranger. She saw a strong thin face behind the spectacles, glossy black hair carefully curled down over the forehead, a firm but mobile mouth. His shoes and clothes were expensive, and he had very clean hands with nicely trimmed nails. He looked to be a real gentleman.

'I take it you are Mrs Kiss then?'

'I am Elizabeth Kiss.'

'That is good,' he said with a smile which revealed white teeth. 'It has taken me a long time to find you. You might be surprised to know I have been making enquiries for you all over West Europe, but perhaps you wouldn't.'

'Perhaps not,' she muttered, secretly wishing her hands

74

would stop trembling, that her heart would cease bumping so. 'Somehow, I thought someday . . . .'

He patted his heavy German briefcase.

'I am here on behalf of a client. Please understand that for a few minutes I cannot mention names, not until I have established your identity beyond doubt.'

'I have my pension book.'

'I need more than that,' he said, taking cream papers from his case. 'Please answer these questions. Take your time, it goes back a long way.'

'Ai,' she sighed in agreement, not taking her eyes from his face.

'Take your mind back to the winter of 1944. Can you tell me what you were doing?'

'My husband and I were refugees. In some ways it seems like yesterday, yesterday I tell you. The cold . . . ai! What cold! Once I heard wolves.'

'You had left your home village and were travelling through the forest?'

'It was the partisans, you see,' she explained. 'A German truck stopped at our farm and an officer came and asked the way to Csejthe. That was enough. Someone in the village – perhaps with a grudge against my father because he was well off – saw the Germans and told the partisans that we were collaborators. One morning my husband and I and our little Kattie – what a happy child she was, God rest her – went to market. When we got back the barn was in flames, the beasts had been driven off and my old father was dead. Ai, ai! The blood. . . .' She crossed herself, making the sign right to left.

'But it must have been God's will. We knew the partisans might return so we left the farm at once, and because of this we escaped a big battle which destroyed the village the next day. We went west towards my brother-in-law's village, a long distance away. It was dangerous to travel by road so we went through the forest. Sometimes we were lost and sometimes snow fell. Whenever it stopped falling we could hear the boom boom of the guns. The cold was so bad it seemed to burn.

'One day we were going through the trees when we came to a little village which had been destroyed. Even God's church was in ruins.'

'Do you know its name?' asked the stranger, his dark eyes gleaming with interest.

She shook her head.

' "We must go on," my husband said. "This is a bad place." In the distance we could hear the noise of tanks, and we ran back into the forest, and then I saw him. . . .'

She paused as visual memory swept her back in time.

'Night was coming on, you must understand,' she continued. 'He was watching us from under a tree. "Stop, Lazlo," I said to my husband. And the little boy came towards us. He must have come from the ruined village because there was dried blood on his face. Perhaps it had come from his mother – God be with her if it was – because I could find no hurt on him. But he was cold, and just wearing an old cloth wrapped round him.

'Lazlo said we must hurry because the tanks were getting closer.

' "We must take him," I said. For a moment I believe Lazlo did not want to, perhaps because we had so little food. But I said: "Lazlo, in memory of our son who was born dead we must take him." So he agreed. And I called him Gyorgy, after our first baby, and I thought: "Perhaps God has given me a son after all."

'I wrapped him up in one of Kattie's coats and he took my hand, but he never spoke. Do you know, he never spoke. But that was not unusual after the bombs.'

Mrs Kiss relapsed into silence. Her memories had become

76

so vivid she almost forgot the stranger leaning forward.

'How long we went through the forest I forget,' she resumed at length. 'It seemed like for ever. And all the time Gyorgy held my hand. He was so thin, and yet he had strength. But my Kattie, who had been such a plump child, seemed to waste away with the hardship. Each morning she was weaker. Then one morning we woke up in a deserted house and she was dead. The same day we reached a DP camp. I carried Kattie's body to it because I could not leave her for the rats in that house.

'At that camp they took Gyorgy away from me – like a stupid I told the Red Cross he was not my son and they took him away. Perhaps at the time they thought I was dying and would not be able to look after him. But it was Lazlo who died, not I. I lived in camps for a long time. When the Communists would not allow the refugees to return, I was allowed to come to this country where I worked as a helper in a hospital kitchen and learned English. I worked in hospitals until I got to be too old. But someday I shall meet Gyorgy again. God tells me that he is looking for me. Perhaps he was taken to America and became a rich man. . . .'

The stranger showed his teeth in an encouraging smile.

'You must understand, Mrs Kiss, that it is very important – very important for you – if you can show me some proof of what you have been telling me.' He waved his documents. 'My client must be absolutely sure that it was you who found the child and that you are not telling something which you heard from some other woman. Did this boy have anything with him?'

'Rags.'

'But did he have anything else – a toy, a doll, anything like that?'

'No plaything, but in his hand he held a piece of metal . . .'

'Metal!' The stranger's voice held a new note of eagerness.

His glasses flashed virescent. 'Tell me about this metal.'

'It was not so big,' Mrs Kiss said slowly, making a small rectangle in the air with her index fingers. 'It was black with tarnish, very old. I think there was writing on it. I put it in the pocket of my coat when I dressed Gyorgy in Kattie's spare clothes.'

'What happened to it, woman?'

'I found it again in the DP camp after the Red Cross had taken Gyorgy away. It had worked through the pocket lining, you see.'

The stranger was on his feet, trying to keep his voice calm.

'And then? Think hard, Mrs Kiss. It is vitally important.'

'But it was just a piece of blackened metal. It had no value.'

'You didn't throw it away? You didn't sell it?'

'Huh, who would want it? No, I kept it, that and a holy ikon I had brought with me. . . .' She gestured to a small ikon depicting 'The Unexpected Joy' whose dark colours were agleam in the light of a little ruby lamp.

'I kept the metal in memory of Gyorgy. I had to remember . . .'

'Then you still have it?'

'Of course.'

'I must see it. It could establish all the proof I need. The little boy you befriended grew up but did not forget you. Now he wants . . . well, first I must examine that plate.'

'Plate? Oh, the metal. It is in my kitchen drawer. Wait, I shall get it. It will take me a little time. My old legs. . . .'

The stranger sat twining his long fingers as he watched Mrs Kiss painfully heave herself up and with the aid of her frame shuffle into a tiny kitchenette.

There came the squeak of a drawer being opened, followed by rummaging sounds, a metallic tinkle and then the wheezing breath of the old woman as she made her laborious way back into the room. In her shaking hands she held an

78

old tobacco tin. She opened it and took out something wrapped in a fading silk handkerchief. Mutely she handed it to him, and there was a look of intense expectation on her face as she watched him carefully unwrap it.

Was this the moment she had been waiting for all these years?

The stranger stepped to the window and pulled back the curtains to see the blackened object better in the daylight. He held it close to his glasses, his breath coming fast.

'This is it,' he whispered.

'You recognize it, then?' Mrs Kiss asked, moving closer and closer with her walking frame.

'Yes. Yes.'

She was close behind him now. He continued to squint at the engraved lettering which appeared faintly through the oxidization.

'If you have seen it before, you can only be Gyorgy,' Mrs Kiss said in a flat tone.

Grasping her frame with her left hand, she withdrew the carving knife from under her old cardigan with her right. Then, swaying as she tried to balance, she held the handle with both hands and raised it high. With an ultimate concentration of her strength, she brought it down in a gleaming arc to pierce the stranger's back. The slender steel vanished with sickening ease into the fabric of his coat.

Still clutching the metal plate, he turned so that the knife handle was wrenched from the old woman's grasp. Frantically she grabbed at her frame. The stranger's glasses slid comically down his finely formed nose, the look of bewilderment on his features dissolved into a rictus of agony and he collapsed on his side. Bright blood began to meander across the Delft pattern of the worn linoleum.

'Ai, ai, I have waited a long time for this,' cried Mrs Kiss, struggling back to her chair. 'But the good God told me you

79

would come. Only after you had been taken from me, Gyorgy, did I see the naked body of my Kattie and realized that you had sucked her life so that you might live.'

With a sob Mrs Kiss sank into her chair. The sobbing continued and then became something more harsh.

When the welfare visitor received no reply to her prolonged knocking, she hurried to the nearby Ladbroke Grove police station. A young constable came back with her and forced the door with professional dexterity. They found Mrs Kiss sitting rigid in her chair, her eyes fixed uncomprehendingly on 'The Unexpected Joy'. She made no answer when the policeman touched her on the shoulder and said kindly: 'What's wrong, mother?'

He turned to the girl.

'Looks like a stroke, I'm afraid. I'll wait with her if you'll go and phone for an ambulance.' But the visitor was pointing with disgust at her crimson footprints on the lino.

Miss Kiss never moved or spoke again, and the congealing blood which dyed her floor remained a mystery.

9

Snails' trails of moisture crawled down the plate glass of the hospital window. As she lay on her special bed, her body encased in the transparent plastic 'lung', Jennifer listened with pleasure to the heavy raindrops tapping the glass. The only other sounds were the hiss-swish of the machine which kept her paralysed lungs working, and the shallow breathing of the other woman in her room.

Wax-faced, the patient lay a slender, unmoving shape beneath the red hospital blankets. Jennifer sensed that, although she lay so still, within her frame physical forces were engaged in a life-and-death struggle to combat the effect of the operation which had siphoned out a malignant tumour.

Staff Nurse Hoskins came in and fitted a new plasma bottle to the transfusion equipment which stood by the bed of the unconscious woman. She bade Jennifer goodnight and continued on her round. Through the partially-open door Jennifer could hear the familiar sounds of the ward settling down to sleep. As she drifted towards slumber her memory strayed back to a day when her ex-fiancé had taken her to the Sussex Downs. On a hilltop they had lain in each other's arms, and while he kissed her she had kept her eyes open watching cumulus clouds harried by a salty sea wind. At that moment she felt she held the whole world in her arms – now those arms were stiff and useless beside her.

She remembered how Roddy had visited her at first and

the unintentional look of repugnance on his face when he saw how she was utterly dependent on the gadgetry of her breathing apparatus. She could not blame him when the visits petered out. He had a horror of sickness, and there could be no future for them.

Everyone had been impressed by the way she accepted the inevitable following those few hysterical hours after the padre had read her the brief note breaking the engagement. How could they know the thoughts that went on behind her now placid features, thoughts that tonight made tears run down her face. Then, her sorrow spent and wishing she had accepted a barbiturate which would have kept dreams at bay, she began to doze.

Jennifer had no idea of the time when a slight sound roused her. By swivelling her eyes she saw the door was slightly ajar. Enough light glimmered from the subdued lamp in the corridor to outline a dark shape by the bed of her comatose companion. It reminded her of a Burmese shadow theatre she had studied in her student days. She thought it was a doctor on his round until she noticed the figure was swaying in a drunken fashion. It raised its hands to the chromium rod on which a plasma bottle was held by a clamp. With a clumsy gesture it wrenched the tube from the patient's arm and to Jennifer's amazement raised it to its mouth. Above the surf murmur of the respiratory machine, she heard the sound of sucking.

'Oh God!' she whispered. 'What are you doing?'

Slowly the silhouette turned. The dripping tube fell away from its hands and dangled from the transfusion stand. It began to advance across the room and there was something about its walk which for a split second reminded the girl of a diver, a languid slow-motion movement. Adrenalin pumped through her useless body, her mind raced and, turning her head a fraction, her lips encountered the mouthpiece of a

82

pipe attached to her life-sustaining equipment.

It was an alarm system. All she had to do was blow to activate an electronic device which would buzz and blink in Sister's office. Desperately she sought to grip the plastic tube with her lips but, before she could exhale a weak breath, a hand reached over and nudged the arm of the pneumatic instrument a couple of inches away from her mouth. Unable to turn her head sideways, Jennifer sensed those two inches meant the difference between life or death.

'Please, don't do anything silly,' she begged in a sibilant whisper.

The intruder made no answer, but dropped out of her line of vision. She knew something very terrible was about to happen. Her only hope was to try to call for help. She waited for a moment until the pressure within the plastic 'lung' was forcing the breath from her so the exhalation would enable her to cry louder. But the sound died in her rigid throat. There was a click as the power supply for the pump was switched off at the wall. For several heartbeats Jennifer was conscious only of the terrifying silence which replaced the rhythmic surge of the machine. Then the standby mechanism, provided in case of power-cuts, began to draw current from the twelve-volt emergency battery, and the hiss-swish recommenced.

From beside her bed came a low, unintelligible mutter as the enemy's hands fumbled over the respirator in a futile endeavour to locate the master switch. Again the paralysed girl tried to summon up the energy to call; but there came a new sound, a tearing sound as teeth bit savagely at the polythene airline through which the fluctuating pressure from the pump forced her chest to expand and contract.

There was a sigh of escaping air as the tube was perforated. The respirator pump continued functioning uselessly for now the pressure in the 'lung' was lost Jennifer was speechless and dying. She had the sensation of falling away from the world – her last thought was of fluffy white clouds sailing across a brilliantly blue sky.

The Metropolitan Police inspector was more sympathetic than Peter Pilgrim had expected, standing up politely when he entered Sister's office in Fleming Ward.

'I gather you know what's happened?' he began.

'I've heard rumours,' Peter answered.

The inspector said : 'Then you probably know as much as me. All I'm certain of is that two people in this hospital were attacked in the early hours. Dr Stromberg, who I understand is here on some sort of semi-official visit, was found in the corridor leading to this ward with a stab wound in his back. The state of his clothing indicated he'd lost a great deal of blood, though there was hardly any on the floor . . . because of his raincoat, I suppose.

'Around the same time a girl suffering from paralysis was killed by someone interfering with her respiratory equipment.'

'Is it true the air supply pipe was bitten through?' Peter asked.

The inspector nodded.

'Incredible as it seems, it was. So, I have one case of murder and one of attempted murder. It's bizarre and I must confess I'm out of my depth.'

'Has Dr Stromberg told your men anything?'

'No. Sir Henry Beresford had him put in the private ward – Millionaires' Row, isn't it called? – where he's having a transfusion. As yet he hasn't been able to say anything coherent. He seems to be in a severe state of shock.'

'He would be if he lost so much blood. I suppose if he was stabbed from behind he wouldn't have seen anything anyway.'

84

'True,' the inspector agreed. 'And no weapon has been found. The surgeon who attended to him said it was a clean knife wound. The knife could have come from the kitchens.'

'We certainly don't have knives lying about the wards,' Peter said. 'But if the attacker was the same who went into the paralysed patient's room, why didn't he use the knife on the plastic air tube? Why bite it?'

'You have put your finger on the problem. What do you think, Dr Pilgrim?'

'Obviously it can only be the work of someone extremely disturbed mentally. We do get such cases from time to time, usually people suffering from certain forms of schizophrenia. They may have hallucinations which cause them to do violent acts. By law, we cannot restrain such persons until they are officially "committed"; I mean we can't tie them up or anything like that.' He gave a ghost of a smile at the way he had expressed himself. The inspector nodded understandingly.

'But if we have a patient who is likely to go berserk we keep a very watchful eye on him. He'd be in a room to himself, and there would be a brawny orderly with him. I obviously don't know all the patients in this hospital, but I know of no cases like that at the moment.'

The inspector pulled out a packet of cigarettes, looked around the white office and replaced them unopened.

'I rather gathered that from other members of the medical staff I've spoken to,' he said with a sigh. 'Tell me, doctor, in your opinion, would it be possible for a patient with schizoid tendencies to get up, carry out his attack and then go peacefully back to bed again?'

'Anything is possible where the human mind is concerned. Having done it once, of course, he would be likely to do it again. Most probably he would be hallucinated and hear voices commanding him to act in this way, perhaps to

85

destroy something evil. In a mystical hallucination – such as some saints have had – he might have thought that Dr Stromberg was the Devil. He might have bitten the air tube because his "voices" told him it was the Breath of God.'

'A plasma bottle had been interfered with. Could he have thought it was the Blood of the Lamb?'

Peter almost smiled. He said: 'Perhaps. As I said, anything is possible. If a patient got up, committed the crime and then went back to bed, blood stains on his pyjamas would soon be noticed. And where would he hide the knife? Nothing can remain long in a hospital without it being seen. They're always tidying up and cleaning in the wards.'

'If only it'd been last week, when I was away on holiday,' sighed the inspector. 'I don't like this one at all. How about the staff?'

'That's probably more likely than the patient angle. A hospital worker, a nurse or a doctor are just as likely to suffer psychiatric disorder as anyone else.'

'Can you think of anyone?'

Peter shook his head, then asked: 'It couldn't have been a child, could it?'

'Doubt it. Why?'

'Just thinking out loud.'

'Really, doctor? You must have had some reason?'

'All right, a little while ago a child patient of mine bit an orderly. It was a nasty bite, and he's on leave to get over it. She's narcoleptic, and a strict watch is kept on her wakeful periods. I'll get the report if you like.'

'Please. No stone unturned and all that sort of thing.'

A minute later Peter returned.

'She's in the clear. She slept right through the night, and she's still asleep.'

'Thank you, doctor,' said the inspector who had brought out his cigarettes unconsciously for the second time. 'If you have any ideas, or hear anything, you'll let me know?'

Peter nodded and walked into the hospital where, despite the efforts of the ward sisters who had been briefed by Matron, the virus of fear was spreading through the circulation of the establishment. The most popular rumour was that a homicidal lunatic was at large. No one wanted to be alone with anyone else. Nurses walking down the long fluorescent-lit corridors started with terror when there was a footstep behind them. A patient by himself in a bathroom would hastily leave if another came in.

Only Old Billy down in the bright white morgue ignored the contagion. When a porter came wheeling in a shrouded trolley, he waved to the coffin-sized drawers in the large refrigerated wall and said: 'At least my customers won't be sticking knives in me.'

He thought his remark so witty he repeated it to everyone who came within earshot that day.

It was the day which was to become known in the history of the London Hospital for Diseases of the Nervous System as Black Friday. As usual Sister was a few minutes early when she came on duty in Fleming Ward. The night staff were finishing their chores and yawning, the day staff were also yawning as they arrived. On the surface routine seemed normal, beneath it Sister could sense suppressed tension.

A day had come and gone since the police arrived to investigate Jennifer's death, but no clue to the killer had been found. In the exclusive private ward at the top of the building Dr Stromberg had opened his eyes and told the inspector weakly that he had no recollection of the attack.

Fearing the killer might strike again (as Fleet Street had put it) policemen, obvious in green porter's coats, patrolled the hospital passages, but nothing abnormal had transpired. Peter Pilgrim, along with his fellow doctors, had spent the night checking patients' dossiers, searching for some hint which would indicate sudden psychotic violence. Not only were the files of those actually in the London searched, but also a vast amount of material relating to discharged patients who would be familiar with the hospital layout. Their work ended abruptly at 8.30 a.m. when an Irish wardsmaid in Fleming went into the men's bathroom suite.

She began sweeping the floor and the cubicles. The door of one of these was closed. She hit it with her knuckles.

'Hurry up in t'ere,' she called impatiently. 'Yers should be finished by now.'

There was no answer. For a while she continued sweeping, muttering complaints under her breath, until there was only the closed cubicle to be cleaned.

'Come on out, will yers,' she cried. 'T'ink I got nuttin' to do but wait for yers.'

There was no answer, so she pressed the door. At first it would not open, but then with a scraping sound (a chair had been wedged against the handle) it swung inwards, and the girl's shriek echoed through the ward. When Sister and a staff nurse arrived moments later the girl was standing outside the door, wringing the hem of her brown uniform and crying: 'Holy Mother of God! Holy Mother of God!'

Pushing her aside, Sister entered the cubicle. In the bath lay Lionel Tedworth. His clothes were folded neatly on the floor. It was obvious he had climbed into a hot bath and cut his wrists. Now he lay up to his chin in pink, cold liquid.

'Holy cow!' exclaimed the Australian staff nurse, looking over Sister's shoulder. Hardened as she was, the sight of the white, drained face with its glaring eyes was too much. She was sick in the washbasin but recovered quickly.

'What can I do, Sister?' she asked.

'I think we'd better pull out the plug,' said Sister calmly. 'You go to the office and phone Matron. Get a nurse to come and look after this wretched girl. I'll stay here until help comes.'

Sister closed the door and was alone with the body of her orderly. As the contents of the bath gurgled out, she bent and picked up a piece of paper which lay on the top of the clothing. The neat block lettering said: 'I am taking this step because in a lucid moment I realize I have done something terrible.' The next line had scribble drawn through it but Sister was still able to decipher: 'The girl in Chalk Farm . . .' The line below continued: 'Something has changed inside me and I am not worthy to live. Please have my body cremated. L. Tedworth.'

So it was him, thought Sister, now running the cold water tap. I wonder how long he'd been going mad? He always seemed a bit too good to be true. God! This is a hospital for nervous diseases and yet we didn't see what was going on under our noses! I wonder what he had in mind for Britt when she bit him. . . .

Her thoughts were interrupted by the breathless arrival of Matron and the police inspector.

He looked at the body professionally.

'Five or six hours?' he said.

Sister nodded. 'He must have come in at the witch hour,' she said. 'Not many people around then. He'd got a white coat, so if any of your men had seen him they wouldn't have been so suspicious.'

The inspector nodded and read the paper Sister handed him.

'That'll be the end of the headlines anyway,' he sighed. 'I wonder who the girl at Chalk Farm was? Probably we'll never know.'

Within minutes of Bernadette Kelly having found the corpse, the news had permeated the entire hospital. At first there was shocked incredulity, but then as the matter was exhaustively discussed it began to seem more possible.

'Of course, he did have a funny streak,' said an orderly who had worked with him in the canteen. 'He was always very efficient and smarmy with the customers, but he had a mean streak if he had it in for them.'

'He hated blacks,' said another. 'Maybe that's why he knifed the foreign doctor.'

'He's not a black. . . .'

' 'Course I never heard him talk about girls. I think he was a bit, you know, odd.' And so in countless conversations Lionel was tried and found guilty. The lunch time edition of an evening paper carried a front page banner: 'Orderly's Suicide at Murder Hospital', but in the next edition it was reduced to a few lines to make way for 'Plot to Kidnap Pope'. By afternoon hospital routine had triumphed and life was back to normal.

Catheterized, tied in a regulation linen shroud and with its nostrils plugged with cotton wool impregnated with eau-de-Cologne, the body of Lionel Tedworth was removed to the mortuary. Old Billy, leering with excitement, supervised its placing in a refrigerated drawer.

'Fancy it being 'im wot done it,' he chuckled delightedly. 'Well, he ain't never done me a bad turn.' It was the opposite – the attendant had earned himself ten pounds by ringing news of the suicide through to a newspaper office that morning.

The porters withdrew and left Billy (nicknamed Charon by some) in charge of his spotless chrome and white-tiled kingdom. Having checked everything was in order, he went into his little side office to return to his copy of *Revue*.

Later that afternoon he looked up to see Dr Pilgrim enter.

'There's a cadaver I want to see,' he said, lack of sleep showing in the paleness of his face. 'Tedworth, from Fleming Ward.'

"Im wot done it,' said Billy, his tongue flicking like a serpent's through his pursed lips. 'Over 'ere, sir.'

He eased a heavy drawer open on well-oiled rollers, glanced at the label tied to a toe of the corpse to make sure it was the right one, then pulled the drawer full out. He watched expectantly as Dr Pilgrim looked down at the blanched features of the dead orderly. From a pocket in his white coat he produced a wooden spatula, forced it between the grey lips, peered closely under the brilliant fluorescent light, then tossed it into a stainless steel surgical bin.

'Thank you,' he said and walked out.

Wonder what that was all about, mused Billy, returning to his paper and the last of a smashing series of articles devoted to the sex life of Copenhagen.

Another dream, another dreamer.

Dim consciousness in the border state between death and life where the bewitched knew not himself, only a glimmering of his condition.

Around him soft blackness. He was secure here, for, beyond the softness, were hard walls which left him safe to dream. To dream until his time would come and he could pursue that elusive longing which, in some old world, had once been quenched.

Memory was rare, and then only a sense of red-streaked dread followed by the well-being of his new modality.

Sometimes the black softness swathing him rocked, but with no effect on his languor, not even when metallic echoes drummed about him.

Then warmth. A warmth so strong the black softness became acrid. Locked in his dream he was unaware of cracking wood and rents which admitted incandescence and the roar of fire, of smoke curling about him and white flames dancing joyously.

Suddenly a moment of realization that the dream was doomed. From somewhere, where he knew not, a cry was wrenched which was the essence of despair. Then dream and dreamer dissolved to dust.

10

'Sit down, Dr Pilgrim,' said Sir Henry Beresford as Peter entered his office which, although it was part of a modern hospital, resembled an old-fashioned study complete with glass-fronted bookcases surmounted by white plaster busts. For decoration there were seventeenth-century anatomical diagrams hanging on the Wedgwood blue walls.

Sir Henry tapped the folder of case histories which lay on his leather-topped desk beside a framed citation for services to medicine. As usual he was impeccable in a dark suit and silver-grey tie, and with his abundant steel-coloured hair brushed severely back he looked exactly what he was, an aristocrat of the medical profession.

'I want to discuss your narcoleptic project,' he said as Peter sank into an over-stuffed chair of buttoned leather. 'I must compliment you on the way you have written your reports. Perhaps it comes from having a literary father.'

Peter smiled obediently.

'It seems you have done everything possible over the past year, yet I fear little positive progress has been made. Indeed it has been an unfortunate project, with your patient attacking an orderly who subsequently ran amok and committed *felo de se*.'

'With greatest respect, I have eliminated several theories and I'm on to a clue which has never been investigated in the past.'

'I agree you put paid to the Bernstein theory,' Sir Henry

conceded, 'but it seems you became side-tracked when you began advancing your ideas about an infectious blood syndrome. Your last paper reads more like an essay on science fiction.

'May I remind you, Dr Pilgrim, that we are in the seventies, that we deal in facts and realities, and that we are medical technologists. If I sound carping it is because you have committed the unforgivable sin of letting your imagination run wild. You have worked with dedication I grant, but I believe your forte lies in psychiatric work rather than in neurology – in that sphere at least there is more than a hint of the witchdoctor.'

As Sir Henry spoke Peter's face flushed and his jaw muscle tensed, though when he spoke his voice was under control.

'You are referring to my suggestion that behaviourism might be passed on through blood?'

'I am. Although you don't say so in so many words, the implication of your summary is positively mediaeval. As you know I believe in absolute honesty between myself and my colleagues, and therefore I must tell you I believe the unfortunate events in Fleming Ward warped your judgement almost to the point of morbid obsession.'

'I merely postulated it might be possible for a behaviour pattern to be passed on through the transference of blood. You must admit the circumstances were unusual. My Swedish patient received a blood transfusion after an accident some time ago in another country. We have no means of knowing where that blood actually came from, yet following its induction into her body her behaviour pattern changed and she became narcoleptic.

'Blood comes from some strange sources these days. Just let me read you this from the *Guardian* newspaper.'

From his wallet Peter extracted the cutting his father had given him at the Soho restaurant. Casting his eye to a passage marked with red ball-point, he said: 'This comes from an article on Haiti published in the *Guardian* last December ... "Other 'liberalization' measures which have been taken by the new Interior and Defence Minister, Roger Lafontant, who succeeded Cambronne, include the closing of a US-run plasma collecting company, Hemo Caribbean, which made vast profits for itself and Cambronne by exporting the blood – and, it is thought, the corpses – of severely undernourished Haitians to US hospitals."

'Now, while I cannot prove there was anything wrong with the particular blood the patient was given, I'm suggesting the possibility of a factor connected with blood which we do not yet recognize or understand ... a psychic influence which is separate from the chemical compounds.'

Sir Henry toyed with his gold-plated Parker.

'When this girl came to England,' Peter continued stubbornly, 'she awoke from a coma and attacked an orderly, drawing blood. Just before that she'd had an EEG which was utterly blank. After the attack the orderly went into coma and I had an EEG done on him – with exactly the same result. Also his behaviour pattern altered disastrously. Later the other narcoleptics, who also had been bitten by Britt, developed a taste for human blood. ...'

With a bleak smile Sir Henry interrupted Peter: 'My dear doctor, in medical research – as in any field of research – there is the danger that when a researcher finds himself on a false track he cannot admit it. He clings to the path of his investigation with determination which in any other field of endeavour would be highly commendable. What is not commendable is the researcher's inability to face the reality of the situation. It leads to a waste of more talent and money than I care to think about.

'Your patient is probably schizoid and as a result suffers from intermittent violence. The fact you mention the blood exporting business in Haiti only confirms my feeling about your ideas. Do you infer this blood comes from zombies?'

'That was only an example,' Peter said, aware he was losing. 'I mentioned it because in some countries it is impossible to trace the origins of supply.'

Sir Henry glanced at the gold face of his watch.

'You suggest the attack on the orderly may have affected his subsequent behaviour,' he continued. 'Equally he might have been an already disturbed man and the shock of the attack was enough to tip the balance of his sanity.

'Another point you raise – melodramatically – is that the narcoleptic children developed a predilection for blood after being bitten by the Swedish child. Utter nonsense! Those young children, suddenly aroused from deep sleep, were naturally excited by the situation. Their curiosity was aroused by the brightly coloured liquid dripping down the wall and they investigated it, not only visually but orally, as young children will. Yet this demonstration of childish curiosity leads you to think they were – and I quote your words – "thirsting for blood". Dr Pilgrim, I find your attitude very unscientific.'

'I suppose when the case is presented as you have just done, and if I was not involved with it myself, I'd be inclined to agree with you, Sir Henry,' said Peter. He felt sick with the growing belief that perhaps Sir Henry was right.

A heavy silence filled the exquisite office, then the knight said in a kindlier tone: 'I have decided we should end the narcoleptic study, Dr Pilgrim. It has proved fruitless. In view of this, I suggest you take some leave to get over the upsetting events which have taken place in Fleming Ward recently. Then we will discuss your future activities with the Lord Foundation who sponsored the programme. Have a good holiday and come back refreshed. And may I add that if I sounded harsh about some aspects of your work, I have absolutely no complaint over the way you have conducted your normal duties.'

Peter rose to his feet.

'Thank you, Sir Henry,' he said, and wondered what the hell he had to thank him for. 'I'll take your advice.'

Walking away down a corridor he saw Anne-Marie hurrying towards him.

'How did it go, Peter?' she asked as they met.

'Dreadful. The project's ended and I'm as good as finished here. I was told to take a holiday.'

'*Sacré Coeur*, what a disappointment for you after all that work,' she said sympathetically. 'But in one way I am glad — you will be able to come on holiday with me now.'

11

The gleaming white cross-Channel hovercraft swept up the Calais beach in a miniature sand storm. The thunder of jet-turbines died to a growl as it settled on its concrete pad and men in blue overalls converged upon it. Soon afterwards Peter and Anne-Marie were driving along the N7, through open fields where farmers plodded behind ponderous, cream-coloured draught horses.

They spent the night in Lyon, delighted to be able to share a room after the segregated life imposed by hospital routine. Next morning, they continued south along the Rhone, crossing the river at the Pont St Esprit to take the road for Arles. After several hours of driving Anne-Marie suddenly clapped her hands in delight.

'Look,' she cried, pointing to the summit of a hill on their left. 'Do you see it?'

'What?'

'That lone tree. When we used to come down here as children my father always used to say: "There you are, *mes enfants*, that is the first cypress – the sentinel of the South."'

As she spoke a yellow car hurtled past them with an arrogant fanfare of air-tone horns.

'My God!' cried Peter. 'Did you see that one go?'

'Yes, and it had a GB plate.'

Half an hour later they were approaching a sharp bend when they saw a gap in the hedge ahead. Beyond it the yellow car glowed in the Mediterranean sun. It was obvious the driver had been unable to negotiate the bend. The car had shot off the road and cut a furrow across a cornfield.

'That was the Aston Martin which overtook us,' Peter said. 'Can't say I'm surprised. Lucky it didn't roll over. I wonder what happened to the driver.'

Shortly afterwards they saw the figure of a girl in green slacks and shirt waving from the roadside. With the sun behind her, her hair shone like burnished copper. Peter pulled up and she began speaking in French, until she noticed the steering wheel of the Citroën was on the right.

'Oh, thank goodness, you're English. I had a bit of trouble with my car – like it's in the middle of a field back there.'

'Are you all right?' Peter asked. 'No bumps on the head?'

'No. Thank God for seat belts. Could you take me to the next village? I'll have to go through the dreary performance of getting a breakdown truck – the old Yellow Peril won't reverse out over that ditch. It's a drag because I'm on my way to Saintes Maries de la Mer.'

'Jump in,' said Anne-Marie. 'We're heading for the Camargue, too.'

'I'd better introduce myself,' said the girl as she settled back. 'I'm Holly Archer, not that I expect that means anything. You don't look like *Revue* readers.'

After they had exchanged names – and while Anne-Marie gave their passenger an appraising look through her oversized sunglasses – Peter said: 'Tell you what, we can take you to Saintes Maries. We'll stop at the next decent garage and arrange for your car to be looked after, and then you can pick it up on your way back.'

'That's great. I'm afraid it'll mean you going back for my cases.'

'That's no problem.'

When they resumed the journey they overtook several caravans being hauled by ramshackle cars.

'The Gypsies are still going south,' said Anne-Marie. 'There's even one walking.' She pointed to a woman trudging along the side of the road with a handcart, her long dress trailing in the dust. When Peter pulled into a garage and Anne-Marie explained to the proprietor in fast French about the Aston Martin, Holly disappeared to the lavatory.

'No wonder she ran off the road,' she said to Peter when the arrangements were concluded. 'She's as high as a kite.'

'She certainly seems to be under strain,' Peter agreed. 'She's talking a little too fast and a little too loud, but it might be the shock of the accident.'

'Don't you believe it,' Anne-Marie retorted. 'It's booze. She probably is one of those alcoholic journalists.'

'She has nice hair anyway,' he said as Holly reappeared.

'That's the most unprofessional comment of your life,' snorted Anne-Marie.

They reached Arles in the rush hour and, after several wrong turnings, found the N570 which ran to Albaron. Dusk was beginning to settle gently over the empty landscape when Anne-Marie said: 'Now we are on the edge of the Camargue.'

Peter flexed his shoulders against fatigue as he drove.

'We've made good time,' he said. 'Holly, we'll take you to your hotel in the town, then Anne-Marie can show me the way to *La Maison des Papillons*.'

The air still held the chill of dawn as Peter and Anne-Marie crossed the courtyard to where the Citroën was parked. The abundance of semi-tropical plants surrounding the ochre-washed house, with its brick-coloured pantiles and blue shutters, brought it home vividly to Peter that he was at last in Provence. He was in a different world from that of the London Hospital for Diseases of the Nervous System with its

100

ugly puzzles and disappointments. The winter of his discontent had been left behind.

'Let's drive into Saintes Maries de la Mer before there are too many people,' Anne-Marie said as she settled beside him in the car. 'There's sure to be one place open where we can get coffee and croissants.'

'I can't wait,' he grinned. He turned the ignition key and the Citroën lurched down the long driveway. Soon they were gliding along a narrow road which curved across the flat Rhone delta. On either side rushes bowed beneath the force of the mistral. Above, the sky had a delicate opal tint foretelling the hot, wash-bag blue which would come once the sun was high enough to start mirages rippling above the salt pans.

'Look,' cried Anne-Marie, actually clapping her hands with delight. *'Gardiens!'*

On the road ahead of them was a line of black figures astride large white horses, the counterpoint to the black fighting bulls the *gardiens* reared. Anne-Marie waved as the car slowed to pass. The youngest rider, proud in his black leather with silver buckles, blew her a kiss. The others nodded their broad-brimmed hats with dignity.

'How marvellous,' said Anne-Marie as Peter accelerated. 'They are the real cowboys, those ones. It was the *gardiens* who went to America ages ago who started the cowboy style there. They are wearing their best, they must be going to the running of the bulls.'

On the road they passed more colourful caravans pulled by a varying assortment of cars, ranging down from an ancient Mercedes, whose rusted mudguards flapped like wings, to a pink Cadillac.

'Not all the Gypsies are poor people,' said Anne-Marie as they overtook the Cadillac. 'Some of the fairground and carnival folk are very wealthy. You'll be surprised at some of the luxury caravans at the encampment.'

Peter noticed a row of people crouched in a line across a field.

'What are they doing? They look like Chinese rice planters.'

'That's just what they are doing, planting rice,' explained Anne-Marie. 'I told you the Camargue is wonderful, Peter. Now you have the proof of what I say. You have seen the cowboys, now you see the rice being planted as in Hong Kong. There are lagoons full of pink flamingoes as in Africa. Tomorrow we must get horses and ride out to see them.'

Peter parked the car by the small church with a battlemented tower, a reminder of the days when the Corsairs came raiding for Christian slaves. They found a little cafe in a square and settled themselves under a Martini umbrella. As he took their orders, the sleepy *patron* told them they were his first customers. Nearby an old man in a clown's costume peddled large balloons which, filled with hydrogen, continuously tugged at their strings. With his free hand he banged a drum and often a Gypsy child handed over a coin and scampered away with a balloon bobbing above it.

When he was opposite them the clown fumbled with some change, dropped it and in the following confusion released the score of strings he had been holding. Immediately white, red, blue, green, and yellow globes drifted skywards amidst the laughter of the spectators.

'That should give him a good subject,' said Peter.

'Mmmmm?' said Anne-Marie.

Peter pointed to the corner of the square where a young artist had set up his equipment. Anne-Marie slipped on her sunglasses and looked in the direction of Peter's pointing finger.

She gazed intently for a moment then muttered: 'Yes,

"Balloons over Saintes Maries de la Mer" should make a good picture.'

Peter watched with interest as the young man set about his work, quite unconcerned by watching Gypsies. He was wearing an old straw hat which reminded Peter of Van Gogh.

After a few minutes the painter straightened up, thrust his hands into the back pockets of his jeans and strolled slowly round the square, looking closely at the buildings and the deep shadows they cast. As he came close to the cafe where Anne-Marie was thoughtfully regarding her cup he paused and looked at her with a slight smile on his finely-chiselled lips.

Peter was used to men looking at Anne-Marie with admiration. Usually it half flattered and half annoyed him, but this made him uneasy. There was something arrogant about the young man's bearing as he stood there, rocking slightly on his heels, hands still thrust behind him. It seemed he was about to say something, then thought better of it and began to whistle. He turned slowly and sauntered across the square to his easel where he continued to rough in with a piece of charcoal.

'Look, there's Holly Archer,' said Anne-Marie suddenly, and for a second Peter thought he detected a note of relief in her voice.

Across the cobbles she came, the sunlight turning her hair into a vivid aureole. She was dressed in a white slacks suit with a bottle-green scarf.

'Hi there,' she said. 'Mind if I join you?'

She, too, wore sunglasses, but they did not hide the tell-tale smudges below her eyes from Peter.

'Sit down please,' invited Anne-Marie. *'Garçon!* How are you today, Miss Archer? No bad effects after your little accident?'

'I'm okay,' said Holly, lighting a Sobranie. 'But what a

103

night I had! The dreams! I thought I was going round the twist! Well, this should put it right.' She put a green and black capsule into her mouth and swallowed some coffee.

'Do you take many of those?' asked Peter.

'Professional interest, doctor?'

'I'm sorry.'

'This assignment is supposed to get me over the abdabs, so let's hope this is the last one. What's in the book for today?'

'The Gypsies are still arriving,' said Anne-Marie. 'The final ceremony won't take place for nearly a week, so you will have plenty of time to relax. They are running the bulls this afternoon. This morning I was going to take Peter along the shore.' She threw Peter a private glance while Holly watched some men begin to assemble a small roundabout in the centre of the square. He nodded agreement.

'Please come with us, Miss Archer,' she said. 'It will help you get over your bad night.'

'Call me Holly, please, and thank you very much.'

They rose and walked down a narrow street to the sea front. A low concrete sea wall ran to the right, and behind it they could see the tops of the caravans in the Gypsy camp. To the left was an expanse of bone-white beach stretching into the shimmering distance.

'It's marvellous,' breathed Holly. 'I'm better already. I can't believe it. Look at those boats.' She pointed to where several high-prowed fishing boats had been drawn up on the fine sand.

'They are decorated the same as when Van Gogh made his picture of them,' said Anne-Marie. 'Only now they have outboards instead of sails.'

'No wonder he came here to paint,' said Peter. 'This light's almost too intense.'

As they began to walk along the littoral Holly said to Anne-Marie: 'Could you give me the background to this fes-

104

tival? I was in too much of a state to bother with research before I left London.'

'Saint Sara, who they worship here, has never been recognized by Rome, but she is still the patron of Gypsies and vagabonds,' Anne-Marie explained. 'The legend is that after the crucifixion the two Holy Marys left Palestine by boat, with their black servant called Sara. Their vessel was wrecked on this beach and the women were cast up, very unhappy and bedraggled. Sara disappeared and returned with stolen clothing for them to wear. From that incident the town got the name of Saintes Maries de la Mer – and the Gypsies their saint.

'For her festival Gypsy families come from all over Europe. They honour her in a way which I think can only be pagan. You will see next week.

'At the moment the statue of Saint Sara, which is about the size of a child and has a black face, is in the crypt of the church. Later we must pay our respects to her. Next week she is brought out for the ceremony of the robes, and then to be carried in procession to the sea. It is very moving to see so much sincerity. When I was little I was brought for the festival from Arles and I got so caught up in the emotion surrounding Sara I howled my eyes out.'

'What's the ceremony of the robes?' Holly asked.

'Through the winter the women of each family sew a beautiful silk robe for Sara in remembrance of when she arrived naked on the shore. Next Thursday she will be brought out on to a platform by the church. Last year's robes will be taken off. Then representatives of each family will lay a new robe on the statue's shoulders. By the end of the ceremony she looks like a huge bundle of cloth.'

While the two girls talked, Peter was content to amble behind and enjoy the harshness of the sun. Ahead were scintillating stretches of dried sea salt, and trembling in the heated air beyond them was a grotesque formation.

'What's that?' asked Holly, squinting through her sun-glasses.

'It looks like the hand of a giant who has sunk in the quick-sand,' Anne-Marie said.

As they drew nearer Peter exclaimed: 'It's a tree which has been washed up, but it could be a piece of modern sculpture.'

'Let's paint it white and sell it to the *Musée d' Art Moderne*,' Anne-Marie joked. Laughing like children, they ran across the rippled sand to the half-buried tree which soon dwarfed them. The action of sea and sand had polished the wood until it was like gnarled bone.

'What a beautiful thing,' Holly said, running her hand over the bleached grain.

'Signorina, please stand there, just as you are.'

They turned at the sound of the unexpected voice.

Running down a sand dune was a man in pale blue slacks and navy sports shirt. Approaching middle age, as testified by the fullness of his belly against his expensive lizard-skin belt, he still moved with speed and grace. His glossy hair was thinning above his high, broad forehead but as compensation it was allowed to curl fully over his collar.

He was brown. Almost *too* brown, Holly thought, though the tan emphasized his even teeth attractively. His most pleasant feature, she decided, was his eyes. As black as olives, they had great depth and a quality of gentleness. Only the thin lips hinted ruthlessness. She had seen the face before, but where?

'Excuse me shouting,' he said, holding up a black 35 mm Pentax. 'I was going to take a picture when you came along. Signorina, as you stood with your hand on the tree it looked fantastic.'

'This for the local camera club?' asked Holly with a bright smile.

'Excuse me again. I take photographs for my living. My name is Bruno Farina.'

My God, thought Holly. Of course!

Bruno Farina smiled and raised his hands in a typical Italian gesture. He had only said a few words, yet already they liked him.

'I'll be happy to be your model,' Holly said.

'It is your hair, signorina. I am taking colour, and it will look magnificent there by white branches with such a blue sky as a background. Excuse me once more,' and he danced forward and without disrespect took a length of Holly's hair and eased it down across her face.

'The windblown look,' he explained.

Peter and Anne-Marie moved back out of range as he began to work and Holly struck attitudes by the natural abstract. With swift dexterity he changed lenses, lay on his back to get certain angles, and raced up a sandhill to get distant shots. Runnels of sweat shone on his wide face. Finally he kicked off his moccasins and, with camera held high, splashed into the light surf to get a picture with foam-flecked water as a foreground. They joined in his laughter as an unexpected breaker caught him. When he rejoined them he was soaked to the waist.

'For such pictures a little wet is nothing,' he said. 'Signorina, you have modelled free for me. So, supposing I make some money out of the pictures, let me spend some in advance. Please, all of you have lunch with me back in Saintes Maries.'

They agreed, and Bruno Farina became their friend.

As they trekked back along the beach Peter and Anne-Marie stooped to collect some tiny but exquisite shells where the froth of spent waves became the plaything of the mistral. Holly and Bruno Farina walked on ahead, hands in pockets and heads bowed with conversation.

'Do you know who he is?' asked Anne-Marie as she reached to pick up a pinkish scallop shell. 'Look, a mermaid's fan,' she added and held it up.

'He's a photographer called Bruno Farina,' said Peter.

'He's *the* Bruno Farina,' she said. 'He's one of the top photo-journalists in the world. They use his work in the colour supplements in England. I often used to see his work in *Paris Match*. No wonder Holly's thrilled to meet him. She fancies him.'

'But she's only just met him, how can you say that?'

'You'll see,' Anne-Marie replied with a mischievous sparkle in her violet eyes. 'If Bruno plays his cards right, as you say, Holly will be able to throw away her pills.'

The central square was now thronged; townsfolk, tourists, hippies and Gypsies all mingled in the dusty heat. The merry-go-round was now whirling to strident carnival music. Gypsy children queued impatiently to ride the red-nostrilled horses which swung out so magnificently at the end of their chains.

Bruno led them to a restaurant where apparently he was already well known. The *patron* greeted him expansively and gave him a table with a good view of the square. As they thankfully sat down to their aperitifs, he continued working. Fitting a 135 mm lens into the Pentax body, he picked it up and aimed at any pretty Gypsy girl he noticed crossing the square.

'I wish I had been a photographer rather than a writer,' declared Holly. 'Click! Your work is done. When I get back I have to write it and put in the angles.'

Bruno shrugged. 'Not so easy as that, signorina. Anyone in the world can pick up a camera and take a picture. Yet why is it that if you have two men with exactly the same equipment, one sells a picture for hundreds of dollars and the other never sells a thing?'

'I suppose it's all in the eye,' Peter suggested.

'You are right, my friend,' cried Bruno, tapping his right eyelid. 'It is the artist's ability to see in a way that makes others see. My father was an artist, from him I get the eye. It is the eye plus the ability to push the button at the exact moment – that is all. But it is hard at first. I started on a Vespa trying to get snatch shots of film stars on the Via Venetia. More competition there than in Vietnam. So I quit, sold my father's paintings, and went to the East where I was determined to stay until I sold a picture story to *Life*. Story after story I sent, my savings became nothing, I lived on rice – and how I hate rice.

'Then I did a little thing on the children's games. Bloody executions, bloody revolutions, bloody wars, bloody earthquakes – nothing! Indian hopscotch, and I was in!'

A waiter brought their *écrevisse* and for a while the talk died. Now the heat drove most of the people from the square; only the ragged children continued to surge round the carousel. An old Gypsy woman, bulging with fat and smoking a short pipe, waddled towards them along the line of umbrella-shaded tables.

'I think she's a fortune-teller,' said Anne-Marie.

'She has a good face, that one,' muttered Bruno, quickly changing lenses again. 'Signorina, please get her to tell your fortune.' He leaned back in his metal chair to get enough focusing distance.

'I'd rather not,' said Holly. 'I don't . . . oh, what the hell! For the great Bruno Farina, why not.'

'You may learn something interesting,' Bruno said. 'Here is *argent* to put in her palm.'

Anne-Marie spoke to the old woman in fast French. She

nodded, picked up the coins from the check tablecloth and turned to Holly. For a moment she looked at her face intently, then took her hand and scrutinized the palm. Her eyes swivelled from Holly's hand to her face and back to the hand. Then she deliberately spat on the palm, threw the money on the table and shuffled away as fast as her bulk would allow.

Bruno swore in musical Italian and jumped up.

'Let her go,' said Holly. Her face screwed up with repugnance and she began wiping her hand with a paper handkerchief. 'The dirty old bitch must be mad!'

'Have a drink,' said Peter, pouring wine from their litre bottle.

'What do you say, doctor? She has the madness, eh?'

Peter nodded, but there was a troubled line on his forehead. Holly continued to scrub at her hand with paper handkerchiefs but soon cheered up enough to attempt to joke about it.

'If my editor were here he'd turn it into a story,' she said. ' "Gypsy's Warning Crossed my Palm with Saliva." '

They laughed their appreciation and Bruno gallantly kissed the hand which had been defiled.

12

The night was hot and still and a rhythmic sighing like the breathing of a giant came from the sea. On its oily swell lanterns of fishing boats cast intermittent reflections. Laughter gusted from the Gypsy encampment, as did frequent outbursts of flamenco. Behind the ancient silhouette of Saintes Maries de la Mer a golden moon climbed over the world's rim.

Peter Pilgrim sat in the still-warm sand, letting a handful hour-glass through his fingers. In his free hand he held a glass of whisky and Perrier. Beside him Bruno Farina did likewise. Anne-Marie had gone with Holly to her small hotel, giving them a chance to get mildly drunk together.

'Bullfighting tomorrow,' Peter said inconsequently.

'Better get there early for a good seat,' said Bruno, helping himself to the bottle. 'If there is an injury you rush into the ring with your little black bag and be a hero to your French lady.'

'I'd already find you there with your little black camera,' laughed Peter. 'I envy you, Bruno. All you need is your camera and you can roam the world, your own master.'

'A lot of jobs seem good to those who haven't got them,' he replied. 'It's only when you're doing it yourself you realize the snags. But compare my erratic way of life to yours. There you are in a modern hospital in a beautiful white gown. "Swab," you say to a beautiful nurse, or "Forceps." And with a skilled movement your save the life of a

Cabinet Minister. "Dr Pilgrim is always so wonderfully cool," whisper the beautiful nurses. But I suppose your work is like all work, it has its disappointments and frustrations.'

'You're damn right there,' agreed Peter. 'I was taken off important research just when I thought I was getting somewhere. I'm still puzzled by it all, and God knows what I'll do in England. Back to some routine job, I suppose.'

Bruno lit a Disque Bleu in sympathetic silence, waiting for Peter to continue. To his own surprise, Peter did continue. He told Bruno about the research into narcolepsy, and – perhaps stimulated by the alcohol, or the presence of a willing listener – described Britt's obsession with blood.

'I can never prove my theories now I've been taken off the work,' he concluded.

Bruno looked sideways at him with great curiosity.

'But if you are right her so-called infection will continue, surely,' he said.

'Yes, I think it has.' Peter went on to tell Bruno about the bizarre death of Jennifer and the orderly's suicide.

'He may have become morbidly interested in blood after the child had bitten him and become unbalanced enough to commit suicide,' he said. 'But I'm sure he was not the one who killed Jennifer.'

Bruno's face was briefly illuminated as he inhaled. 'How can you say that?'

'There was something I seemed to remember about him, so in the morgue I examined his mouth and found his dentures had been removed. No one with false teeth could have bitten through a tough plastic tube. It would have needed real teeth, and strong and sharp ones at that.'

'What does that mean?'

'That this *infection* – that's the only word I can use to describe this neurotic taste for blood – had spread further

112

than the poor bastard of an orderly. It must have spread to someone else at the hospital.'

'But if there was someone who had bloodthirst, why should they cut off an air supply to a paralysis victim?'

'There was another patient in Jennifer's room. She was in coma after an operation, and was having a transfusion at the time. After Jennifer's death, it was noticed the plasma bottle had been interfered with. I believe the latest victim of the *infection* came into the room after the blood in the transfusion bottle. When he or she realized the girl in the "lung" could see what was going on he or she killed to silence her.'

'Were you working in an English hospital or the *Grand Guignol*!' exclaimed Bruno. 'I'm pretty used to the sensational, but this. . . .'

'I know it sounds insane,' admitted Peter, his voice slurring slightly as he held up the bottle to the moon to see if there was any whisky left. Reassured, he poured himself more. 'The fact remains Jennifer was killed in a macabre way, the ward orderly committed suicide out of self-disgust, and someone stabbed Stromberg. . . .'

'Who?'

'Axel Stromberg was a specialist visiting our hospital,' Peter explained. 'He was stabbed the night Jennifer died.'

'What a story,' said Bruno with admiration. 'It sounds too far-fetched though I'm sure you're telling the truth.'

'That's what my superior said. I think he believed I was heading for a nervous breakdown or something. . . .'

'Axel Stromberg,' mused Bruno. 'Where have I heard that name?'

'It's well-known in neurological circles. He's got a clinic in a remote part of Finland where he studies cases of extreme psychopathy. Some of his ideas are quite revolutionary.'

Bruno shrugged and lay back on the sand. Already Peter

113

was regretting he had said so much and the Italian sensed this.

'Ah, the world is still a mysterious place,' he said in order to close the subject. 'I believe the more man learns the more he realizes how much there is still to be understood. When God is finally reduced to an equation man will find that by knowing everything he knows nothing.'

'A profound paradox.'

'Yes,' cried Bruno, sitting suddenly erect and slapping Peter kindly on the back. 'But we should not be profound on such a night. Lo! 'Tis the gala night . . . and we should be dancing with our women.'

The four friends arrived an hour before the bullfight was due to start and just managed to find places on the warm cement seat above the barrier. This red wooden wall was built a short distance from the curving side of the arena. It allowed favoured enthusiasts to stand looking over the top, or for anyone hard pressed in the ring to leap over it to safety.

Flags fluttered above the amphitheatre, 'Carmen' music blasted from loudspeakers, vendors shuffled among the ever-increasing crowd and two old men in white coats raked the sand with great artistry. Peter noticed the straw-hatted artist had taken a seat in the highest circle and was now busy with a sketching board on his knees. Something restrained him from mentioning it to Anne-Marie.

Exactly on time a taped trumpet fanfare echoed and two riders trotted into the ring. Astride Camargue thorough-breds, they were dressed in old-fashioned Provençal costume.

'One of them's a girl,' cried Holly. 'Oh, I must get an interview with her – women's lib in the bullring!'

'There's nothing to stop women taking part,' Anne-Marie

said. 'In this contest the winner is the first to plant a rosette on the neck of the bull. Do you see those spear things they are carrying? They do not hurt the bull, they only hold a rosette which has a little spike so it can be pinned to the bull's thick hide. As soon as it's placed, a ribbon is released from the lance which streams behind the rider so the crowd know a strike has been made.'

There was another metallic fanfare and a black bull ran into the ring. Greeted by a roar of approval he stood tossing his head defiantly in the centre.

'An old one,' whispered Anne-Marie to Peter. 'He's probably been in the ring dozens of times and knows all the tricks.'

The girl rider spurred across the ring in front of the bull. His head lowered, his tail went high and he charged. It took no urging from the girl to make the horse gallop. As the bull followed closely she turned elegantly in her saddle and, leaning back over the rump of her mount, thrust the lance over the horns of the bull and tried to touch his neck. But the horse turned at the wrong moment, the chance was gone and the bull returned to the centre.

The other horseman trotted towards the bull with poised lance. Already Peter could enjoy the skill of horse and rider, and the extreme grace with which they moved. He also appreciated the cunning of the bull who refused to tire himself once he realized he was not going to catch the fleeing steed. Sand flew as the two animals sped round the ring, the rider turning in the same manner as the girl in a fruitless attempt to plant a rosette.

When the circuit of the ring was completed, the girl rode at the bull to attract his attention. Again she moved with grace, her plaited hair flying from under her stiff-brimmed hat. Beneath her black waistcoat the traditional lace shirt appeared dazzling in the fierce sunlight. It was obvious she was the favourite by the way the audience cheered as she deliberately slowed her horse and once again turned for the lance thrust. Again the bull veered out of range.

So the contest continued. From the benches cine cameras ticked as tourists zoomed in on the contestants. A sheen of perspiration covered Bruno's broad forehead as he continuously focused, shot and wound on.

The girl changed her tactics. Instead of allowing the bull to chase her and hope for a backwards thrust, she rode straight up to the beast and, as he lowered his head, her lance flashed down. A flower seemed to bloom on the animal's neck and the girl spurred to safety with twenty feet of scarlet ribbon floating from her lance tip.

Similar contests followed until ironical cheers greeted an announcement over the loudspeakers.

'Now's your chance,' said Anne-Marie. 'Anyone can try. Look at those Gypsy lads jumping into the ring.'

When a score of men were in the arena a fresh bull was released. There were roars of laughter as the would-be matadors hastily retreated to the other side of the ring while the beast surveyed them arrogantly. A rosette was fixed between his horns, and the prize went to whoever could snatch it. The event was really a piece of buffoonery to amuse the spectators.

A lean Gypsy seemed to be the only serious contender. Again and again he approached the snorting animal, but each time the bull shook its head and turned on him. Once the bull's shoulders sent him crashing to the sand. Luckily there were so many in the ring the bull could not concentrate for long on any particular foe.

'I must get in there,' muttered Bruno and next moment Holly saw him leap over the wall, haul himself over the barrier and join the heroes of the ring. The Pentax, fitted with a wide-angle lens, was in his hand.

'He's mad, I say mad,' wailed Holly.

Suddenly the fun went out of the afternoon as the bull swung round and tossed the lean Gypsy so his face struck the edge of the barrier. Bemused, he slid down the boards to the sand. Meanwhile the bull veered and caught Bruno. The Italian hit the barrier with his head and arm simultaneously. Stewards in white jumped into the ring and lured the bull from the two huddled figures. Three *gardiens* trotted into the arena and guided the animal out, but before the bull had gone Peter was by the two injured men. The Gypsy sat holding his cheek, bright blood oozing between his fingers. Bruno was unconscious.

Peter bent over his friend, probing with experienced fingers. A moment later Anne-Marie was beside him.

'Is he all right?'

'Organs and ribs seem okay,' said Peter, continuing his rapid diagnosis. 'Don't like the look of that arm, could be fractured.'

Bruno's eyes flickered. He looked at the sky and swore in Italian. Peter pressed him back when he made an effort to rise.

'Take it easy, Bruno,' he said. 'You may have concussion. Anne-Marie, please get the Citroën round to the entrance. We'll drop the front seat and take Bruno to the Arles hospital. I want him x-rayed at once.'

'What can I do?' asked Holly as Anne-Marie ran off.

'Have a look at the Gypsy,' Peter said. 'I think it's only a small gash.'

Holly went over to where the young man still held his face. As she approached he made the sign of the cross with his bloodied hand.

'Are you all right?' Holly asked in French.

'I don't need you,' he retorted.

'Don't be silly,' she replied, taking some paper handkerchiefs from her handbag. 'Just let me look at your face. My friend is a doctor and he'll soon help you.'

'I don't need you,' muttered the youth, attempting to rise. Ignoring his protests Holly bent over him and began wiping away the blood. There was a clean cut along the cheekbone.

'It's not deep. I think all he needs is some antiseptic and a plaster,' she called to Peter. A stretcher had been found and Bruno was carried to the entrance to await the Citroën.

'Bring him to the car,' Peter told Holly. 'I've got my bag in the boot.'

Behind them a fanfare sounded and the bullfighting resumed. Anne-Marie drove up and lowered the front passenger seat while Peter attended to the Gypsy's face.

'Not bad enough for stitches,' he declared. He sprinkled the wound with sulphonamide powder and strapped a dressing in place with a couple of pieces of sticking plaster. The youth said: '*Merci*,' and walked away quickly.

Meanwhile Bruno was lifted gently and laid on the reclined seat. Anne-Marie put the tartan car rug over him.

'Do you mind if I leave you here?' Peter asked Holly. 'There's only room for one in the back and as Anne-Marie is a nurse...'

'That's all right,' Holly replied. 'If they keep you in I'll come and visit you,' she added to Bruno.

'Thank you, signorina,' he murmured with something of his old smile. 'I would take it as a favour if you could collect my camera equipment.'

'Of course.'

The blue car swung away from the entrance and Holly stood alone in the hot square, abstractedly licking her finger. Behind her cheers rose from the amphitheatre as though nothing had happened.

13

Holly sat alone at a cafe table in the square by the church of Saint Sara. A glass of brandy was before her. Over the cafe terrace small bats whirled in the mercury glow of a street lamp. Within three Gypsies made sad music with violins and an accordion.

Stubbing out her cigarette in a Cinzano ashtray, she swallowed a green and black capsule with the remains of her drink.

'*Garçon, encore s'il vous plaît.*'

Only the impassive waiter could say how many drinks she had taken. Holly knew she was being foolish, especially taking tranquillizers with spirits, but she excused herself because she was in a state of nervous tension.

It was partly the shock of seeing Bruno laid out in the bullring, partly the fears and nightmares of the last weeks coming to a crescendo within her head. She had no one to turn to. Peter Pilgrim and his girl friend had not returned from Arles. The advent of Bruno had made her begin to believe her problems were coming to an end, but now. . . .

Strange, she thought as she focused on a pinpoint of light reflecting amber in her drink, he is not hard-boiled. Someone with his international reputation ought to be steel-hard, yet he seems almost childish as he jokes and bounces about with his camera.

A man appeared from the shadows. Holly recognized the Gypsy whose face she had wiped after the accident. He swaggered past, paused, winked slowly and jerked his head in the direction of the shore.

Oh God, no! she thought and ignored him pointedly.

He repeated the invitation and then moved away, his step unsteady. She thought: I'm not the only one who's on the vino.

From the church came a low chanting, contrasting with the shrill Gypsy music in the cafe, and a procession led by a priest and an altar boy carrying a cross wound into the square. Each member carried a candle and the night was so still the yellow flames hardly flickered.

I wish I was religious, thought Holly. Wish I'd lived in the days when religion was a very real part of life. No need for psychiatrists then, the confessional was much better. She reconsidered: Hell no! I'd have been burnt at the stake. And she laughed out loud. A family group at another table looked round curiously.

Am I starting a breakdown? she wondered. People have them often enough, but what actually happens to them?

The procession shuffled to the dark side of the square, and all Holly could see was the line of lights. As she watched it seemed to tilt and fall away. It kept falling over and over as she tried to focus her eyes.

I'm just plain drunk, she decided. I'm drunk and morbid, but tomorrow it'll be all right. Bruno'll be back and I'll be all right.

She asked for *l'addition* and was surprised to find how much she owed for brandy. She fumbled with her purse, paid generously and began walking to her hotel, unaware of a shadowy figure following her.

At the hotel entrance she squared her shoulders and walked carefully into the foyer but the desk was deserted. Distant laughter from the kitchen suggested the staff were having an impromptu celebration. Gratefully, Holly went to

120

her room, flung herself on the bed and dozed.

The shattering of glass jerked her awake. She blinked at the jagged hole in the window and for a moment could not comprehend what had happened. Then her eyes travelled slowly to the mat on the tiled floor. Warily she approached the dark shape lying on it. It was a black cat.

'Pussy,' she whispered, wondering if the animal had dashed itself against the window pane. 'Poor pussy.'

She touched it carefully with the toe of her shoe, but instead of the expected softness she felt the rigidity of rigor mortis. Holly's scream was stillborn in her parched throat. Pussy had been decapitated.

She backed to the door and ran down the corridor. Lights burned, but the foyer was still deserted. There was no one to help her, and the hotel had become an evil place. She ran out and hurried down the street towards the sea. Air and space were what she needed. As she stumbled along she was racked by sobs.

The town was still reassuringly alive, but she wanted to avoid the strangers in its streets. She felt sand beneath her feet and her shoes filled with water as a wave creamed the beach. She turned and followed the shore in the direction she had taken with Peter and Anne-Marie a few days before.

Gradually the sobbing ceased. She lit a Sobranie with a Stick lighter Bruno had given her that morning. After she had used it, she held it like a talisman. The noise of the stay-awake cafes was replaced by the comforting pulse of the sea. She sat down, her arms hugging her knees and her eyes fixed on the luminous surf.

Suddenly she knew she was not alone. She looked up and saw the Gypsy standing near her. The moonlight bleached colour so he appeared a monochrome figure against a contrasting background of white sand and black sky.

'Go away,' said Holly. She repeated it in French.

'I only want to thank you for what you did for my hurt,' he answered in slurred French. He squatted down and watched her.

'What have they got against me?' she asked at length.

'Who?'

'Your people.'

'*Alors*, they are crazy,' he said, his hand roving over the plaster on his cheek. 'It is the old woman. She is crazy, I tell you.'

'What does she say, the old woman?'

'That you are *upier*.'

'What's that?'

'She is crazy, I say. She and the other old ones. They are still back in the ancient times. She says she saw it in your hand.'

As he spoke he moved nearer.

Holly held her palm close to her eyes.

'It's just an ordinary hand.'

'I think you are very pretty,' said the Gypsy. 'I think you need a man.'

She shook her head.

'I see the way you look at me,' he said, moving again. 'You want a real lover, not that Italian. Gypsy men know how to give much pleasure to women.'

'Please go away.'

'Hey, what are you saying? Why do you act like this? You wanted me to follow you. Why do you come here with me? For what? For talk?'

'I didn't know you were following me. I've had a shock.'

'You want money, eh? You're a whore, eh? You think you can fool with me because I'm Gypsy, do you, English whore?'

He was close. His winy breath disgusted her.

'Go away,' she repeated. 'Or I'll shout for help.'

He laughed, stood up and looked down at her.

'I'm going to give you what you want, English whore.' He took his hand from his pocket. There was a snap and a murderous switch-blade reflected the moon like a slender icicle.

'Do as I say or I mark you,' he hissed.

Holly tried to rise to her feet but he sent her sprawling with his left hand. He stood straddling her and laughing quietly. Carefully he folded back the blade and unbuckled his belt.

Lying on the sand Holly was hardly conscious of the rhythmic shock to her body as the Gypsy squirmed on top of her. His breath rasped in her ear, his long oily hair lay across his mouth, beneath his chest his hands tore at her. As the rape continued – no, it could not be called rape, there was no resistance from the dummy spread-eagled by the sea's murmuring margin – her mind was liberated from the confusion, fears and doubts which had tormented her for so long.

If, during a space-walk, an astronaut's umbilical line broke and he drifted away in the grip of some gravitational current he would have the impression his spacecraft was falling from him into black infinity. So Holly felt the world fall from her, leaving her scattered thoughts weightless to crystallize into a new dimension of awareness. And, as she suddenly *understood*, a cry forced itself from her throat.

The pumping of the automaton stopped. The Gypsy looked down at her with a sneer of victory on his sharp features.

'So, after all you like it,' he said. 'You like a Gypsy lover, eh? I give you more yet.'

She sat up and regarded him in the merciless moonlight. No longer a creature of menace, he had shrunk in her eyes

123

to something pathetic. 'Boy, now it is my turn,' she said.

He glanced about, half fearful of the unexpected strange vitality radiating from the English girl. Still holding his hand she led him back along the beach. By now the street crowds had melted away and as they approached the hotel they were seen by only a couple of tipsy violinists making their instruments lament beneath a street lamp.

'Wait,' said Holly at the hotel door.

She walked into the foyer and found it still deserted. She returned for the Gypsy, confident he would still be there. Now his bravado was gone he was hers.

In her bedroom she calmly picked up the headless cat and threw it through the window. The Gypsy looked round nervously as though he was unused to rooms. Holly stood by the bed.

'Come, Gypsy.'

He stepped forward obediently and faced her. In the glow of the bedside light he had a mesmerized look.

Holly smiled at him and ran her fingers softly over his face. They tightened on the sticking plaster and tore it off. The Gypsy gave a grunt of pain, and with the gash reopened blood trickled down the brown skin.

Holly put her arms round his neck, pulled his head to her and began to kiss his cheek. As she did she felt his body tremble, then shake convulsively as though racked by fever. He raised his arms and embraced her. Together they rolled in slow motion on the bed, Holly's mouth still caressing his wound.

14

The dark statue of Saint Sara stood on a platform constructed against the church wall. Smiling Gypsies milled before her. This was their occasion. This afternoon they ceased to be stateless vagabonds wandering from fairground to fairground, they were an ancient people united in the adoration of their saint. Townsfolk and tourist sensed this and kept in the background. Hot silence filled the square.

With sibilant encouragement from her mother and aunts, a small Gypsy girl climbed the platform steps and stood before the image with a pink cape. She held it for Sara to see, then placed it about her shoulders.

A shout and hand-clapping followed, and the ceremony of dressing Sara had begun. The child kissed the kiss-worn face, which was level with hers, and scampered to her family. A little boy, bearing a mass of embroidered blue, was pushed forward.

'I don't see Holly anywhere,' said Peter to Anne-Marie on the edge of the crowd. 'You'd have thought she'd have found us if only to hear how Bruno is getting on. When I told him he'd have to stay in for observation he asked me to drive her over to Arles, but how can I if she's disappeared?'

'There's probably some explanation,' Anne-Marie said, on tiptoe to see above the heads of the crowd. 'Perhaps she has taken a bus to Arles and is with him now.'

On the platform the face of the saint took on a pink hue

from the lipstick of the Gypsy girls and women as they gave her their annual salutation.

Peter and Anne-Marie watched for a while, then he said: 'I think I've seen enough, darling. Let's go to our cafe and have a beer.'

'I've been waiting for you to say that.'

After the intense light of the early afternoon, the interior of the cafe was dim and cool. As they pushed through the multi-coloured strips of plastic door curtain Peter and Anne-Marie found it had a strange underwater quality and, because of the ritual outside the church, it was almost empty. Thankfully they sat at a corner table and two glasses of Stella Artois were brought.

'I'll bet poor Bruno is furious at having to miss this,' said Anne-Marie, dabbing froth from her lips.

'In the ward he begged me to bring him back,' Peter said. 'I had to explain very carefully about the danger of delayed concussion. I'll find out how he's progressing.'

At the zinc-topped bar he bought *jetons* and at the wall telephone put a call through to Arles. After some erratic work by the hospital switchboard, he spoke to the sister of Bruno's ward. There was a puzzled look on his face as he returned to the table.

'Was your French up to it?' she asked.

'Only just. The sister said he was out in the grounds but he'd left a message for me. Would I take Holly to see him. So, she hasn't gone to Arles.'

'Strange.'

'That girl worries me, taking those damn tranquillizers with alcohol. Remember how she was when we picked her up on the road? She's on the verge of something nasty.'

Anne-Marie gave a little shrug.

'You are not your brother's – or your sister's – keeper even if you are a doctor.'

126

'I know. It's just that in the few days we have been here we all seem to click together like some sort of temporary family.'

'You're right. Buy me another drink and then we'll go to Holly's hotel.'

Later when she rejoined Peter outside the hotel it was Anne-Marie's turn to look puzzled.

'She's not there. They were so guarded I think something strange is going on.'

'Ugh,' she exclaimed a moment later. 'What's that?' With her shoe she indicated the bloated body of a headless cat in the gutter.

Friday arrived, and the fervour generated by the previous heat-dazed days of the festival seemed to explode in a crescendo of emotion. Just before midday the procession began to form in front of the church door. In one corner aloof *gardiens* in their finest black suits patted the necks of restless horses. In another a score of small choir girls in mediaeval costume were marshalled by their teacher. Their role was to follow the mounted guard of honour singing ancient chants of the festival.

'Did you ever see anything like it, Peter?' asked Anne-Marie as they surveyed the sweating block of humanity. To get the procession organized seemed to require a babel of advice and curses. A fierce argument raged as to who would have the honour of carrying the saint. Tourists edged dangerously along wall tops to get photographs and there was uproar as one fell on the packed bodies below.

Bells boomed in the church tower and Peter and Anne-Marie heard a universal gasp of delight as Saint Sara – a black be-diademed head above a bundle of silken mantles – was borne into unaccustomed sunlight on a litter. *Gardiens* swung into their cowboy saddles and walked their mounts forward, the choir fell in behind and miraculously the procession began to wind away down a street. The litter was followed by hundreds of sweating Gypsies so tightly pressed there was danger of some being pushed through shop windows.

'Sara . . . Sara . . . Sara . . .' they shouted in unison. Sometimes there were scuffles as devotees struggled to touch the saint's silk cloaks as the litter swayed past.

By cutting through an alley Peter and Anne-Marie were able to take up a position in a neighbouring street to watch the procession approach. As the *gardiens* jingled past, a man with his left arm in a sling moved out and, holding a camera in his right hand, knelt to photograph the little girls in their black and white-lace gowns.

'Bruno!' cried Peter. 'What the hell are you doing here?'

He skipped out of the way of the advancing litter-bearers and smiled. 'I broke parole.'

'You're crazy,' said Peter. 'After that crack . . .'

'I'm all right, doctor,' Bruno said. 'A bit weak I admit, but okay. I had to come today otherwise the assignment would be lost.'

'It takes nearly an hour for the procession to go round the town,' said Anne-Marie. 'Let's take Bruno somewhere to rest. He'll need to be steady to get his shots on the shore.'

Leaving the near-hysterical chanting, they found a small bar and Bruno gratefully sat on a metal chair.

'Where's Holly?' he asked while Peter tapped the zinc counter with a coin.

Anne-Marie raised her shoulders and said nothing.

'She must be around somewhere working,' muttered Bruno unhappily. 'She's on an assignment, too.'

At that moment Holly was in the almost deserted post office. Fumbling for her most valuable asset as a journalist – her contacts book – she said in French: 'Please, I want to send a telegram.'

When she had completed the message and paid the teller, she walked unsteadily down an empty street to the east end of town. The sound of the procession came faintly to her ears.

It's out of my hands now, she thought. I have found the strength, but it is out of my hands now.

She left the town by a road which cut through the sand-hills behind the wide shore. With her rumpled clothing and the sick pallor her Hampstead friends might have had difficulty in recognizing her. Only the halo of red-gold hair was the same. But she had no thoughts for them, only the Gypsy whom she had arranged to meet at an old fisherman's hut far along the beach.

At the edge of the sea, a mile east of Saintes Maries de la Mer, the world went mad. As the procession wound over the quivering shore *gardiens* spurred into the waves and, when their horses were belly deep, turned and faced the land with their bull tridents raised. The children's choir scattered as the tight column behind the saint suddenly dissolved and Gypsies rushed into the water with ecstatic faces. Still the shouting continued: 'Sara . . . Sara . . . Sara . . .'

Stumbling over salt-encrusted sand, the delirious litter-bearers approached the sea. They paused only to adjust their grips, then waded into the water. Gypsies converged about them, splashing with their hands so droplets rained like diamonds on the figure of the saint.

What pre-Christian ritual they perpetuated they knew not; all they cared was that this was the orgastic finale to the festival, the ultimate homage to Sara. Their cries of exultation sent gulls screaming out over the waves.

For a minute the shouting and splashing continued and the saint's outer cloak lost its sheen as it absorbed the spray.

Then the bearers turned and reeled to the shore. *Gardiens* moved forward and flanked them.

There was a sudden silence, a post-coital *tristesse*. Slowly men and women left the water and trudged back to their camp without speaking. Even the children were quiet.

Saint Sara was borne back to the town but the procession had shrunk to a mere handful of people.

The warped hut smelled of tar and fish. Holly lay on a pile of netting and gazed at the vivid blue framed by doorway. Occasionally the breeze brought the sound of 'Sara . . . Sara . . . Sara . . .' With a trembling hand she opened her box of black cigarettes and lit one. Her hand might shake, but inside she felt calm, strong, and curiously content.

The Gypsy appeared against the sky. He entered and crouched in the sunlight which streamed through the door. All he could see of Holly in the shadows was the tiny eye of her cigarette.

'There is trouble,' he said in French. 'When I went to my caravan this morning my wife saw the marks you had left on my body. When I slept she crept out and told the old one, who is her aunt. They knew I had been with you. Someone must have seen us go to the hotel. Now the old crazies say I am *upier*, too.'

'Does it matter?'

'You do not know Gypsy custom. It is bad enough my wife's father knows I have dishonoured her, but this . . . this . . .' He waved his hands weakly. 'Why did you do this thing to me, woman?'

Holly laughed.

'Who took me at knife point, Gypsy?'

'I am a good man to come and warn you. I should have left before the festival finishes. I am in terrible danger, and you are too. You have money. Perhaps you can get me away. I am poor.'

'What is the danger?'

'You from England would not believe. I know little of it, but once long ago in Italy . . .' He shuddered. 'It is bad even to talk of it. Let us go away.'

Holly drew on her Sobranie, and said nothing.

'Of course I know it is all crazy,' continued the Gypsy, afraid of the silence. 'I do not believe this *upier* talk of the old ones. It is just that you have strange ways of making love. But the old crazies believe in it.'

'Do you remember last night?'

'I remember it as I would remember a dream.'

'You found it exciting?'

'As exciting as death,' he answered and she laughed at his words.

'I shall get you away, Gypsy, but you must earn your fare.'

'Anything, but let us go now.'

'There is no hurry. The bus will not leave until tonight. And there is no other way. Wait with me, and when it is dark I will go with you to the bus and pay your fare and give you money.'

He nodded gratefully.

Slowly Holly stubbed out her cigarette on the dirt floor.

'Come here,' she commanded. 'We will see if you remember last night's games.'

The Gypsy made a slight whimpering sound. 'Please, I am exhausted. I have nothing more to give.'

'That is not true,' said Holly softly. 'You have more to give me than you know.'

He shuffled towards her on his knees. He kept his head bent and his eyes closed as she undid his shirt and ran her hands upwards over his ribs. A look of pain crossed his sharp features.

'I still hurt,' he murmured.

'Pain can be pleasure,' Holly answered. 'It is something hard to learn, but you will see.' The tip of her tongue dampened her dry lips.

15

Anne-Marie rubbed her palm wearily across her forehead.

'Headache?' asked Peter.

She nodded. 'The heat I suppose, and the excitement.'

'Like me to run you to the *Maison*?'

'Oh no, you can't leave Bruno by himself.'

They were sitting on the side of a gaily painted fishing boat above the tideline opposite the town.

'I'll be all right,' said Bruno. 'Who knows, Holly may turn up.'

(At that second Holly was lying on the body of the sobbing Gypsy, her mouth unnaturally vivid.)

'You stay in Saintes Maries with Bruno and have supper with him,' said Anne-Marie, 'and I'll drive to the *Maison* for a couple of hours of sleep. I'll pick you up at the restaurant near the church after supper.'

Peter agreed and, with a smile at both men, Anne-Marie started in the direction of the Citroën. As they watched her slender figure dwindle over the sand Bruno said softly: 'The doctor has much woman there.'

'The doctor has,' agreed Peter. 'But the doctor is worried, there's something the doctor doesn't quite understand.'

'That makes two of us. Signorina Holly cannot have left the town without seeing me.'

(At that second the Gypsy was trying to free himself from Holly's embrace, but in the stifling heat her moist flesh stayed glued to his. 'You empty me,' he moaned.)

The two men sat in moody companionship, Bruno smoking Disque Bleu cigarettes and Peter making abstract patterns in the sand with his canvas shoe. Both had absorbed the melancholy which pervaded the town now the festival was over. When the sun neared the horizon and turned the lagoons of the Camargue into mirrors of blood, they quit the boat and went to the restaurant by the church for an early meal.

Bruno ordered calvados and they continued to drink it after their meal. Since his arrival in France Peter had drunk much more than he was used to, but he was not prepared for the effect of the pungent spirit, unlike Bruno who took it in his stride.

'It may be a while before Anne-Marie picks me up,' Peter said. 'I think I've more than had my ration, but you carry on.'

'I'll drive you home so you are not too drunk to keep her company,' Bruno said. 'My Fiat's parked at my *pension*.'

As he drove from the sad town they saw a group of Gypsies briefly illuminated by their headlights. Several carried shotguns.

'Where can they be going at this time of night?' Bruno asked.

'Now the festival's over they're probably off poaching,' Peter answered.

A few minutes later Bruno pulled up at the two bougainvillaea-covered pillars flanking the drive which led to *La Maison des Papillons*. Peter walked unsteadily down it to the courtyard before the old house. As he stepped on to its paving he froze.

Anne-Marie sat with downcast eyes on a wrought iron seat with the young artist Peter had noticed wearing the Van Gogh hat sprawled beside her, one hand on her shoulder while he talked low and persuasively. At the sound of

Peter's footsteps on the terracotta tiles she looked up.

'What are you doing here?' she demanded accusingly.

There was such a note of guilt in her voice he felt the hairs on his neck prickle. It was ridiculous: he did not know what to say. Finally he asked: 'Who have you got with you?' It sounded so pompous, like a husband who had found his wife's lover under the bed.

Anne-Marie cast a furious glance at Peter. The artist stood up and thrust his hands into his back pockets.

'I do not know who you are, sir,' he said in Sorbonne English. 'But you seem to be acquainted with my wife.'

'What?' Peter said stupidly.

'It looks to me,' said the artist, picking his straw hat from the bench, 'that there's going to be an embarrassing scene so I'll stroll back to town. Goodnight, Anne-Marie, I was starting to enjoy our little chat, but we'll meet again. Goodnight, Mr – er . . . I'm afraid we haven't been introduced.'

He walked whistling down the drive.

'Peter!' Anne-Marie cried.

'I'm sorry,' he said. 'I've had a lot of calvados. I don't seem to be taking this in.'

'Listen while I explain . . .'

'Tell me, Anne-Marie, is it true what he said?'

'Yes, Peter, I am married to Alain.'

He stood blinking at her in the soft light from a lamp on the wall. He kept rubbing his mouth which seemed to be suddenly parched.

'That seems to be that, doesn't it?'

'Peter, listen . . .'

'It is no use saying "Peter, listen", Madame whoever-you-are. I've enjoyed your company since I've been taking you out but I'm sorry you could not have been more honest with me. I suppose I was useful as an escort while you were in London.'

135

'Peter, Peter,' she interjected, coming up and holding his arms hard above the elbows. 'You must listen to me. It's very important you do, otherwise . . .'

With the slow-motion dignity of a drunk he pushed her away, and said: 'No, you listen to me, Anne-Marie Clair . . . is it Clair? Whatever you are going to say will not alter anything. I don't give a damn that you got married before we met. What I can't bear is the thought you never told me. Your bloody silence lied. You knew what I was feeling and you never said a word. No wonder you never wanted to talk about the future.'

He was so distraught he turned from her.

'Peter, I know what you were feeling. I felt it too, I still do. It was because of that I didn't tell you. I was afraid it would make some difference. I wanted to get it sorted out, get my divorce so I would be free to marry you – supposing you would have asked me.'

'You talk about divorce, but why did he follow you to the Camargue?'

'You must understand, I've known Alain since I was a girl. Through my teens I worshipped him. He was a romantic student and he began taking me out when I was sixteen. He was the only boy friend I ever had. I thought I was in heaven when he asked me to marry him. Then . . .'

'Save me the bleeding-heart stuff,' Peter sneered. 'Whatever you say, he still came down here.'

'I am probably richer than you realize, Peter. At least, my father has made a lot of money. Alain's only interest is in money. His parents had none, and as a painter he makes nothing. He found out I was here and came to ask for cash to get out of debt. And he told me how much he would accept for a divorce. He wants to open an art gallery. . . .'

The calvados was burning in Peter's throat and stomach,

136

his pulses throbbed angrily, adrenalin secreted into his blood stream added to his sense of intoxication. There was something so reminiscent about this scene he found breathing difficult. Above all he suffered with a sense of outrage. Why did she have to hurt him?

For a while they talked at each other, neither listening, while a ballet of moths danced about the lamp.

Suddenly Peter said: 'No more talk. I'm going.'

He strode towards the house. She tried to pull his arm. He swung his right hand and hit her on the side of the face. She looked at him with horror. The act filled him with horror, too. It symbolized something snapping between them. Whatever the explanations, things could never be the same now.

Angry with her for causing him to act so boorishly, he stumbled up the steps to his room, flung clothes into his suitcase and panted to the Citroën. There was no sign of Anne-Marie. He put the suitcase in the boot, scrambled behind the wheel and turned the key. He reversed so fiercely the car nearly hit the wall, then he straightened the wheel and accelerated down the drive with gravel spraying from the tyres.

Reaching the road he swung north, only just remembering to drive on the right. As the minutes passed he calmed slightly and tried to concentrate on driving. All he wanted to do was escape back to England. He would think about it all then.

The scene with Anne-Marie brought back another scene; the scene when Marian told him she was leaving their flat to get married. She too had used him, used him as a crutch after her own marriage had collapsed. They had lived together, waiting for the time when she would be over her black depressions, waiting for her divorce, waiting for the good times to come. But when she could laugh again and the divorce was granted, she found someone else to share the good times with.

Once again he had hoped for love, but again the world he had been building up was destroyed in one quick scene.

'Marian . . . Anne-Marie . . . Marian . . . Anne-Marie . . .'

Endlessly their names passed through his mind in a monody as the road passed endlessly under the lights of the Citroën.

16

The Gypsy slowly opened his eyes. Through the doorway of the hut he saw the sky had turned from blue to blood red. Silhouetted against it the woman smoked one of her black cigarettes.

His body ached and in places there was pain, yet at the same time he enjoyed a voluptuous languor. He was not sure what had happened to him. As before, the memory of phrenetic love-making had become dreamlike. It had been more than love-making. He wondered if he had been drugged. Had she secretly given him something those hippies used?

The Gypsy had had much experience with women. During the summer holiday periods there had never been a shortage of foreign girls anxious to learn what a Gypsy had to offer. He looked back on earnest Americans, cynical English and frantic Scandinavians, but none were anything like the strange woman who now sat smoking against the sunset sky. She was . . . reluctantly the word rose to the surface of his mind . . . *upier*?

'It is over,' he said sombrely.

'What is over?'

'The festival. Now they will come looking for us.'

'You are afraid.'

'Yes.'

'Wait until tonight.'

He lay on the roll of net and watched the sky magically

change to indigo. Once the sun had gone night came quickly to the Camargue.

'You have money with you?' he asked in sudden panic. 'They will be watching your hotel.'

She nodded but said nothing.

In the hot silence he tried to understand what had bewitched him. There was the bullring and the pain when his face hit the edge of the barrier. Then this woman with the flame hair had wiped his face and there was something about it which excited him. He had followed her along the shore and had taken her roughly, but after that memory became distorted. It was like looking at himself in old Gabriel's tent of mirrors at the carnival. Everything seemed to swim into grotesque shapes. The only clear recollection was the screaming of his bitch of a wife when he tugged off his shirt in the caravan.

'Come,' said Holly. 'It's dark. We'll be safe in the night.'

He rose reluctantly, fastened his belt and felt in his pocket for the reassurance of his knife.

In the feeble lamplight the streets of Saintes Maries de la Mer were almost forlorn after the festival. A few remaining visitors at cafe tables saw groups of Gypsy men stalk past quiet and sullen. The carnival spirit had left them and strangely there was not a Gypsy girl or woman in sight.

As Holly and the Gypsy walked the narrow thoroughfare towards the square where the bus departed, they were aware of a malign atmosphere. The Gypsy shuddered and glanced anxiously over his shoulder.

'It is bad,' he whispered. 'It is bad.'

'What can they do to you in the town?' Holly demanded.

'You do not know. They would take us away. . . .'

As he spoke three Gypsies appeared at the far end of the street. They stopped, pointed to the couple and called: 'Josef,

Josef!' There followed words in Romany which made the youth tremble.

'Run,' he cried to Holly and, grabbing her hand, began loping back down the street. The Gypsies shouted and gave chase. But Holly had only been dragged a few yards by her panic-stricken companion when a knot of men emerged from the shadows ahead of them.

'Down here,' Holly said, pointing to the mouth of a small alley. The Gypsy's panic infected her and together they bolted over the cobbles.

The alley curved and entered a square. They crossed it and raced down a dark street towards the shore. Houses dropped away and there was the crunch of sand beneath their feet. Small breakers washing the shore appeared as irregular lines of phosphorescence. Fortunately for the fugitives the moon had not yet risen, and beyond the town darkness pressed heavy on the flat landscape.

They raced along the damp sand close to the water. After a few minutes Holly slowed.

'Let me get my breath,' she begged.

He stopped, listening with his head cocked. The only sound was the hiss of the sea.

'Come,' he said. 'We must keep going.' But he too was winded and they continued at a walking pace for half an hour. Then the Gypsy paused.

'Let us go inland before the moon comes,' he said. 'As soon as there is enough light they will ride along the beach on horses.'

'But what will they do?'

For an answer his finger crossed his throat, but in the darkness Holly did not see the gesture.

Leaving the shoreline, they trudged up the sliding dunes until the ground became firmer and Holly found they were walking over coarse grass. The Gypsy gave a terrified cry as he blundered into an old fence of sagging barbed-wire. They climbed it and stumbled on. From the right came the murmur of water from a reed-bordered drainage dyke.

A pale aurora heralded the moonrise. Beneath their feet the ground was becoming soft and marshy, and from it rose tall clumps of rushes. Several times water squelched into Holly's shoes. As the moon edged above the horizon, they saw the water of a lagoon gleam ahead of them. A gentle breeze made marginal reeds sigh sorrowfully.

'Over there,' the Gypsy said, pointing to a low black shape which, as they approached it, materialized into a crude shelter opening on to the water. It was a hide for bird-watchers built on piles.

Gratefully Holly climbed in while the Gypsy cut armfuls of rushes with his knife. These he laid on the plank floor to make a bed. Together they stretched out and, with their arms round each other like frightened children, drifted into uneasy sleep while tiny ripples from the lagoon whispered beneath them.

When Holly woke the early sun was dyeing the lagoon pale pink. Wraiths of pearl mist drifted across its surface. To the right of the hide a group of black cattle were drinking. She was cold, stiff and hungry. Feeling in the pocket of her jacket, she was relieved to find she still had cigarettes. As she lit one the Gypsy opened his eyes and groaned.

'We must go,' he muttered, rubbing his eyes. 'They will soon know we are here.'

'How?' Holly asked.

'That old fat one. She has the sight.'

Holly shrugged.

Leaving the hide, they walked along the margin with wildfowl fluttering at their approach. Nearby was a low embankment with a narrow road running along the top. Some distance away they could see the grey outline of an angler, still as a Chinese figurine with his rod drooping over the water. His motor scooter was parked on the raised road.

'Come,' whispered the Gypsy. He led Holly up the slope towards the machine. On the other side of the embankment they saw a plain patterned with patches of dried salt; crossing it was a small band of horsemen, not *gardiens* on white horses but Gypsies astride Gypsy nags.

Holly's companion ran silently to the parked Vespa. Swearing under his breath, he turned the twist-grip throttle wide open and kicked the starter. After a couple of tries the two-stroke motor clattered into life.

Pushing the scooter off its parking stand, he pulled Holly on to the pillion seat. He clicked into gear and, with the machine swaying alarmingly, they lurched down the rutted road. As the shouts of the angler came faintly to their ears, the Gypsy actually laughed.

'We will beat them yet,' he shouted into the cold air streaming past.

For half an hour they jolted erratically over the narrow roads which snaked over the delta. When they reached a proper highway he turned eastwards and, with the speedo needle quivering round the 100 k.p.h mark, raced towards Arles.

After crossing the Rhone they entered the streets of the old city where the Gypsy skidded to a halt by an early pedestrian.

'La gare, s'il vous plaît?'

With much gesticulation the old man explained three different routes, but as they approached the station the Gypsy braked with a suddenness which nearly threw Holly off. On the steps of the building lounged several Gypsies who, when they saw the Vespa, ran to where an old green Renault was parked.

The Gypsy turned the machine and shot down a side street. After jolting through a maze of *pavé* thoroughfares, they found themselves on a minor road running into the countryside. The Vespa engine howled as the throttle was held open as far as it would go. Holly clung in physical terror to the grab handle in front of the pillion seat. Minutes later the motor coughed, died and the scooter rolled to a silent stop.

Cursing, the Gypsy unscrewed the petrol cap.

'*Merde!*' he cried. 'It is almost empty. We have the reserve, but it is for a few kilometres only.'

He bent and turned the emergency supply tap.

'We will go up there,' he said, pointing to a low mountain surmounted by the ruined citadel of Les Baux. Once a centre of rebellion, it had been blown up with gunpowder by order of the famous Cardinal Richelieu.

Soon they were labouring up a steep road which led to the winding valley whose tortured rock formations were supposed to have inspired Dante to write his 'Inferno'. The fuel ran out just before they reached the entrance to the desolate stronghold. Muttering with impotent anger, the Gypsy dismounted and pushed the machine over the edge of the road. It careered down the slope and smashed itself against a windworn boulder.

Down the valley, where the road curved round a natural castle of rock, Holly caught a glimpse of the green Renault which had been parked by the Arles railway station.

'Quick, up there,' said the Gypsy, his face pale beneath his tan. 'There are plenty of hiding places.'

It was still early in the morning and Les Baux was deserted. At the top of the path leading between the tourist shops the turnstile was unmanned. Climbing past it, the couple began running up the slope towards the cream ruins. The breath hissed painfully through the Gypsy's mouth.

'I am so weak,' he complained. 'Where has my strength gone?' Holly took him by the arm until they reached the

144

towering rock from which the fortress had been hewn. They panted along old paths between roofless walls, to where steps led to the topmost ramparts.

'We'll be safest up there,' said Holly. 'If we can hide until tourists start arriving we'll be all right. They can't do anything once people are about.'

He nodded and began to ascend, hauling his heaving frame by means of the rusted hand rail. They crouched low behind crumbled battlements so they would not show themselves against the sky, and traversed a section of block-built wall to a chamber hollowed out of a natural crag. Here the Gypsy slumped down with his back against the cold stone. On one side lay the ruins of the citadel; on the other an emerald stretch of grass sloped to the edge of a cliff which fell away to an ochre plain dotted with olive trees. Halfway between the wall and the cliff edge was a monument to the Provençal poet Mistral, surrounded by an iron railing. A strong wind blew across the plain from the Camargue and, deflected by the tremendous cliff, moaned eerily over the ramparts.

Holly looked out of a small embrasure. Far below she observed six miniature figures and even at this distance she could see two carried guns and one held a pitchfork. Beneath her fascinated gaze they toiled up to the first tier of ruins and then halted. One looked up, cupped his hands to his mouth and shouted: 'Josef! Josef! Josef!'

In the little rock room the Gypsy shuddered as the echoes picked up the cry: 'Josef .. Josef .. Josef ...'

'We'll be trapped here,' he whimpered. 'They can smell us out like dogs.'

'Keep your cool,' Holly said. 'It'll take them hours to search Les Baux.'

Cautiously she looked down again. The man had vanished into the labyrinth of roofless buildings, cellars and shattered walls. Then she saw a black beret bobbing close to the steps which led up to their hideout. The Gypsy saw it too.

'I'm not going to be trapped here,' he muttered. 'Look after yourself, woman.' He ran out of the chamber and, forgetting in his fear to conceal himself below the crenellation, raced to the stairs. A cry echoed from below as the pursuers spotted him. The Gypsy disappeared from Holly's view and for a few minutes everything was unnaturally quiet.

When she saw him again he was on the outside of the wall, on the grass expanse which sloped towards the cliff edge.

He halted by the monument to Mistral, clutched the railing and fought for breath. Then he turned and his knife flashed in the sunlight. By leaning over the stone parapet, Holly saw a menacing semicircle of Gypsies move slowly towards the youth. As the six men drew close, he moved back from the obelisk and down the slope.

He flourished his knife and shouted. Romany words came faintly to Holly, but a moment later his cries of defiance changed to pleas for mercy. The ring tightened, and step by step he retreated. Now he was in a crouched position, his knife held out in front of him. He dared not take his eyes off the pursuers.

Holly almost shouted a warning as he backed down the increasing incline towards the cliff edge. The men began to move quickly. The Gypsy brandished his knife, and stepped back into space.

For a fraction of a second Holly saw the doll-like figure with threshing arms and legs arc out over the plain, then the edge of the cliff hid it from view. The Gypsies ran to the brink and gazed down.

She knew this was her chance. Bent double she crept along the top of the wall and descended the long flights of stone stairs. With pounding heart, she followed the pathway between the ruins to the open ground which sloped to the unattended entrance. A few minutes later she was running down the road which wound along the steep valley wall.

The Renault backfired into life when Holly was on a stretch of road flanked by a sheer drop on the left and a towering cliff on the right. With her lungs pumping in agony and sweat pouring into her eyes she staggered on. She heard the car skid to a stop somewhere behind her. Three Gypsies jumped out. Then the car jerked forward and swept past her to brake again a hundred feet ahead. The other half of the party climbed out and barred the road. She was trapped between the two groups who had begun their silent, unnerving advance.

She could see their faces now: swarthy, furrowed, moustached features of harsh old men to whom pity could mean nothing but weakness. She could only escape them by leaping to her death. Instead she cowered against the rough rock of the cliff and watched with horrified fascination as one man took a hatchet from the pocket of his tattered coat.

They formed a crescent about her, and she caught the garlic of their breath. The sound of a distant car seemed unnaturally loud. Seconds stretched into eternity as each seemed to be waiting for someone else to make the first move. Or was it they relished the look of stark terror which made her face so ugly?

The spell was shattered by a howl of an Alpine car horn and a Mercedes roared up the road, scattering Gypsies and screeching to a stop with smoking tyres.

The rear door burst open and a tall man leapt out. He pointed a blue steel pistol at the men now huddled at the edge of the road and spoke rapidly in some language unintelligible to Holly. They shuffled their feet nervously, the two shotguns were dropped. One crossed himself, and the tall man laughed.

The dark-skinned chauffeur turned the car expertly on the

narrow road. When the bonnet pointed down the valley the man beckoned Holly and, with his automatic still levelled at the ragged tableau, led her to the Mercedes. The driver leaned back and opened the door for her. The stranger followed her in. The door slammed and the accelerator was pressed to the floorboard. Wheels spun for a second, then the heavy car shot away.

One of the Gypsies retrieved his gun and fired after it, but the pellets pattered harmlessly against the shiny boot.

'Stromberg,' Holly murmured as her eyes rolled and she fainted.

'You called and I came,' the tall man said.

Dr Peter Pilgrim had reached Vienne when radio bulletins first carried the news of a Gypsy's accidental death at Les Baux and the mysterious disappearance of an English journalist from Saintes Maries de la Mer. But he was too preoccupied to listen to the radio.

17

In the bar of the Mason's Arms Tudor Owens asked: 'And what are you going to do with yourself now, boy-o?'

'Not sure yet,' Peter Pilgrim answered. 'It's clear there's no future for me at the London. I might do some locum work until I get things straightened out, or I might go out to the Middle East to see my sister.'

'Look, I have a contact at an abortion shop,' Tudor said. 'I could put in a word for you. Make your bloody fortune, you would. Old chaps out of retirement are making a couple of hundred pounds a week just doing the anaesthetics. There's more money in terminating life than bloody saving it.'

'And while you're around there'd be no shortage of patients,' Peter joked. 'Now, what's been happening since I left?'

'Old Beresford got his computer. Your narcoleptic group has been disbanded. The kids went back to their local hospitals.'

'What happened to Britt?'

'Her father took her back. I heard Stromberg talked him into sending her to his clinic after Beresford pulled you off the project. Stromberg left soon after you went on holiday, swanning round Europe I should think.'

'He's in Finland,' Peter said. 'I picked this up when I collected my things today.' He handed a letter to Tudor dated a week earlier.

The envelope was postmarked 'Ivalo'. Unfolding it, Tudor read:

Dear Doctor Pilgrim,

As you know I was very interested and impressed with your work into narcolepsy when I had the pleasure of visiting the London Hospital for Diseases of the Nervous System, and it was a disappointment to me when I learned your research had come to an abrupt end. As you may know, such research runs parallel to work I am undertaking at my clinic in Finland, and it is my wish to commence a similar project.

Therefore I am writing to inquire if you would be interested in setting up a similar scheme for me. I know that Lapland probably does not hold many attractions for a young person such as yourself, but at this time of the year the weather is excellent, and if the idea of the Arctic Night is unacceptable to you, I suggest we arrange a short term contract of between three or four months.

Your remuneration would be comparable to your English salary plus an allowance to compensate for you having to live abroad.

As time is of the utmost importance, I would be obliged if you would communicate with me as soon as possible. I might add that you would find my clinic suitably provided with the latest equipment, and situated in a delightful position on the shore of Lake Inari.

Sincerely yours,
Axel Stromberg.

The signature was written with an extravagant flourish.
'I told you he was poaching when he came,' said Tudor Owens triumphantly, handing the letter back. 'Are you in-

terested? It would mean you could carry on with your work.'

Peter shook his head.

'Not really. It looks like just a setting-up operation. If I went back to research I'd want to follow it through all the way.'

They talked for a few minutes longer, then Tudor looked at his watch and sighed: 'Duty calls. It's been good to see you again, boy-o. Keep in touch.'

The two doctors left the pub. Tudor walked towards the looming bulk of the hospital while Peter reluctantly drove to Harrow-on-the-Hill.

It was two weeks since he had arrived back from France. Not wishing to stay in London, he had driven straight to Northumberland to visit his father. Although he was determined not to pass on his problems, especially as his father was nearing the end of a book, Ambrose immediately sensed his son was deeply troubled.

When he made a tactful inquiry, Peter answered that it was general disappointment because his term at the London had been ended, coupled with the fact Anne-Marie was now in France. Ambrose nodded and said: 'Sometimes you must look at life as a military campaign, Peter. Do not worry if you sometimes lose a battle – what's important is winning the war.'

When Peter admitted he was unsure of his plans, Ambrose said: 'Why not go out to Abu Sabbah and see Julia on her excavation site? I believe she's close to an exciting find.'

'That's a thought,' Peter agreed. 'I haven't seen her for over a couple of years.' But inside him he knew that whatever he did would not relieve the pain he felt over Anne-Marie.

While Ambrose worked doggedly at his IBM, Peter would walk across the fells. Trees, which earlier had provided delicate black lace fringing for horizon and hilltop, were now transformed by spring foliage, but Peter did not notice them. Remorselessly his mind roved back over that dreadful parting with the French girl. He loathed himself for the way he'd handled it, especially for hitting her; yet when he thought how she'd kept her marriage from him he was filled with anger.

Once, in an impetuous moment, he scribbled on a coloured postcard of the Roman Wall: 'Wish you were here.'

It was then he realized he did not know her Paris address. It was ridiculous, but she had never needed to give it to him, and he had never bothered to ask for it. All he could do was address it to *La Maison des Papillons* with 'Please forward' written across the corner. He walked to the village of Gilsland where he posted it at the small friendly post office.

A moment afterwards he regretted it. What would Anne-Marie think when she received such a banal communication? And did he really wish she was there? What he wanted back was his *illusion* of Anne-Marie, not the Anne-Marie with the sneering young painter of a husband. They were probably back together in a Paris flat by now....

The human mind has infinite capacity for self-torture, and as such ideas occurred to Peter he found he was no exception. He also realized his morose state was worrying his father and affecting his work, so he drove south to London where he officially resigned from the London Hospital for Diseases of the Nervous System – to the satisfaction of Sir Henry Beresford who was allergic to 'cranks' on his staff.

When Marian left him, Peter had moved to quarters provided for single doctors by the hospital. He had kept their flat standing as it was, the mortgage being automatically taken care of by a banker's order. The bother of selling off furniture and having to conduct would-be buyers through rooms which had once been home to him and Marian was distasteful. Now he was returning to it because he had nowhere else to go.

Twilight was gathering as he parked on the forecourt of the impersonal block built on the lower slopes of Harrow Hill. Holding a plastic carrier bag of groceries, he climbed the stairs to the flat on the top storey. As he opened the door he was greeted by a mound of advertising mail and a stale, airless odour; and when he walked down the passage to the kitchenette he found everything coated by a fine dust.

I'm like Julia breaking into some old tomb, he thought.

He put down his groceries and entered the living room. It was familiar and at the same time alien. In the bedroom blankets and sheets were still rumpled as they had been when she left the bed for the last time. A dried stain at the bottom of a cup represented the final cup of coffee she had drunk under his roof. Curiously his sorrow over Anne-Marie was emphasized by this vivid reminder of earlier pain.

To exorcise the memories the silent flat had conjured up, he heated water in the kitchenette for a cleansing operation. Squirting detergent into the sink, he began by cleaning the cutlery which still lay in it. As he picked up a spoon he saw the initials 'M + P' scratched on the handle.

She must have loved me when she did that, he mused. Strange I never noticed it before.

An hour later there was a knock at the door. Peter, his face streaked with dirt, opened it to find Bruno Farina standing with an Alitalia bag in one hand; in the other was a bottle of Bells in the wrapping of a duty-free shop.

'Bruno,' cried Peter. 'You could not have arrived at a better time!'

'How is the doctor?' smiled Bruno, walking in. 'I flew in today. I got this address from the hospital.'

'Great. Let me make you some coffee. I'm just having an almighty spring clean. How's your arm?'

153

'Still a little painful, but it is no problem.'

'What brings you to London?'

'I am on to something bloody big, Peter,' said the Italian gravely. 'I have come to ask your help. Before I begin, get a couple of glasses. We are going to need this Scotch.'

When his tumbler was half filled he said: 'Peter, I was sorry to hear about you and Anne-Marie. I saw her just before she left Saintes Maries. She was *triste*.'

'Was her husband with her?'

Bruno shrugged and repeated: 'I am sorry.'

'It's all right,' Peter said. 'Happens all the time. How about Holly?'

'We will come to her in time,' Bruno said sombrely. 'She's mixed up in this – this thing.'

He pulled a crumpled packet of Disque Bleu from his suede jacket pocket.

'In my time I have done many big picture stories,' he said reflectively, leaning back on a comfortable off-white sofa which had once been the pride of Peter and Marian. 'I got the first pictures out of Kubee, I found Admiral Hart-mann in Venezuela, I got a world exclusive on the Mothers of Life commune in California. I got some of the last pictures of Papa Doc. Those were nothing to what I'm on now.'

'It must be good.'

'Good! It may be sensational as a story, but it's also evil in the old-fashioned sense of evil. And I have a very personal reason for wanting to see it through.'

'Where do I come in?' asked Peter.

'You'll see. Be patient please, this will take some time to tell. Pass your glass over.'

'You say it's evil. I must say, with some practical experi-ence of psychiatry behind me, evil is usually just an attitude of mind.'

Bruno gestured with his hands.

154

'Just listen,' he said. 'Do you know what happened around the Camargue after you left?'

'I did read somewhere about a Gypsy being killed.'

'That's right. He fell off the cliff at Les Baux. At the same time Holly disappeared.'

'Has she been found?'

'No, but after some detective work, I have a good idea where she is. I have many good contacts in the news agencies, and for the last two weeks I have been fitting the jigsaw. There are still some pieces missing, but a picture is emerging.

'After the festival I was worried because I had not seen the signorina. I went to her hotel and they were worried too. She had not returned on the night of the festival, and there had been no word from her. After I slipped some francs to the receptionist, I was told that the night previous to her disappearance a man had stayed in her room with her. I inquired around the town and found she had been seen with a Gypsy – the same Gypsy who had fallen to his death at Les Baux. The local *gendarmes* told me he must have slipped over the edge, it was considered to be an accidental death. But there was something about it I did not like.

'Back at the hotel I paid some more francs and saw Holly's room. I went through her belongings and found her passport was not there, but I remember she carried it in her pocket, as some people do. I also found this.'

From his airline bag he took out a tiny cassette and a miniature black and grey Philips recorder.

'I had to buy this "electronic notebook" to hear the tape,' Bruno explained. 'Holly was a great one for recording her notes. This tape was a sort of diary going back some months, mixed up with story ideas.'

He fitted the one-inch-by-two cartridge into the tiny machine and pressed the finger control. Peter leaned forward

155

as Holly's husky voice began to whisper from the tinny speaker. Bruno turned the volume wheel with his thumb and the words became clearer.

'. . . *Copenhagen has shaken me completely. I don't know what I expected, but whatever it was it was nothing like what happened. I remember leaving the theatre in his car . . . who would believe me? My God, wolfskin seat covers and a negress driver . . . I have no idea where the room was, I was dazed and over-excited . . . cannot remember anything clearly now, it's looking back on a dream after one has been awake several hours. Did he mesmerize me? No, that would be an excuse, I was more than willing . . . I think he sensed I was a virgin. Funny, I don't remember the pain, but afterwards there was blood everywhere. It seemed to drive him crazy, everything blurred but I know I've never experienced anything like it. Could sex have the same effect as LSD? It occurred to me he was some sort of pervert but I didn't care . . .'*

The words faded as though she had held the machine too far from her mouth, then the tinny voice came back: '. . . *the marks on my body. Why am I recording this? I suppose I'm trying to get some sense out of it all.'*

Peter looked curiously at Bruno, wondering what effect these words were having on the Italian if he really had fallen in love with Holly.

'*I had no idea how long I was at that place . . . wave after endless wave of pleasure, utterly utterly intense . . . must have slept at times . . . Yes, I did, but dreams seemed to take over and continue the conscious experience . . . times I didn't know whether I was dreaming or awake, the pain only increased the ecstasy . . . Am I some sort of monster? Was I scared before because I subconsciously knew once I started I'd be like this? . . . Am I some sort of nympho? If I am I don't care, I don't care, I don't care . . . understand the joy*

156

*of martyrs now . . . want to rest now for a long, long time.
They gave me odd looks when he brought me back to the
hotel, must have looked damn white . . . Keats understood . . .*

> *And this is why I sojourn here
>   Alone and palely loitering,
> Though the sedge is wither'd from the lake,
>   And no birds sing.*

*Alone and palely loitering, that's me. How the hell am I
going to do this damned series after that? Bugger* Revue *. . .
going to sleep for a week. . . .'*

There was silence for a few seconds.

Then Holly's voice came more briskly, saying a date, then:
'*. . . back in London a week now. Haven't missed my
demon lover as I expected. Guess it was just a couple of
days of madness . . . maybe I was hysteric, but some of it
must have been real . . . marks beginning to fade . . . the
Copenhagen story is a big success. . . .'*

A laugh.

'*Wonder what he'd say if he knew the real Copenhagen
story . . . let him think of a headline for that one! Back to
cell therapy today . . . Story idea: "I left him at the altar" –
interviews with half a dozen girls who opted out at the last
minute . . . Went to Gloria Simon's reception at the Dorch,
plenty of booze but nothing in it for me . . . Wish I could
sleep, must get some pills or something. . . .'*

There was another pause, then some notes she had recorded for some article she was working on. After another
date the voice continued in a strained timbre: '*. . . dreadful
dreams. Does it go back to Copenhagen? Same old nightmare about bleeding to death . . . maybe understandable, the
curse came on time so I'm not pregnant . . . funny, never*

157

*thought about that at the time ... must get fixed up now I'm
a woman of the world ... God! What would I have produced
if I'd clicked....'*

A shaky laugh.

More work notes, almost indistinguishable because of a
radio playing in the background, then silence. Still without
expression, Bruno turned the cassette over. Now the voice
was shrill: *'... am I going mad? God, if I have that dream
again I'll find a psychiatrist ... Elizabeth says she knows a
good one in Welbeck Street and she ought to know, by God
... what did the devil do to me? No, I can't blame him. It's
something in me ... pills don't help....'*

Pause. Click.

*'Jeff took me to Trader Vic's, super meal ... brought me
home and made a pass ... why not? I'm a woman now ...
but it was awful. He just got me to bed and ... and I got such
an urge ... I was after his blood all right, like the latest
dream coming real ... I threw him out before I lost control
... must have thought I was mad. Bang goes a friendship
... Oh God, I will go to Welbeck Street.'*

The next recordings related to her work, but Peter was
aware of the heightening tension in her voice. Then: *'...
saw terrible accident in the street, blood on the road hypnotized me ... policeman had to lead me away, thought I was
in shock – little did he know ... Welbeck Street seems
promising, but explanations about traumatic first experience
and hymenal blood too glib ... helps during the day, but he's
started coming back when I sleep ... sometimes I almost
decide to contact him ... he said someday I would....'*

A pause.

A date, then: *'... going to Provence. God, I need the
break ... something dreadful will happen if I don't get away
... tablets useless ... thirst so strong bought a pound of
raw steak, made me vomit ... why did I ever have to meet*

Stromberg? Perhaps a priest. . . .'

Peter started at the name and threw a look of inquiry at Bruno who switched off the recorder.

'What does it mean?' he demanded.

'I think you can guess.'

'Bruno, I'm afraid I'm starting to.'

18

'Before we allow ourselves to come to conclusions let us go a little further,' said Bruno, placing the small recording machine on the coffee table beside him. 'From this tape we know Holly met a stranger in Copenhagen with whom she shared some fantastical sexual experience which affected her so much she was heading for a nervous breakdown. About a month ago she got an assignment to cover the Camargue festival, by which time she was living on drink and tranquillizers.

'At Saintes Maries de la Mer she had a little respite from her troubles. She met us, and I think, without flattering myself, she became fond of me. Listen to this.'

He picked up the Philips. There was a jumble of sounds, then Holly's voice came through clearly. For a while her words were verbal notes on the Camargue which she would use later for her articles. Then: '. . . *Bruno is one of the kindest men I've met. How easily I could love him. I am so tempted, especially when I forget the curse that seems to hang over me. At times I think he could save me. But I must not involve him . . . I thought I was getting over it all, but when he kissed me tonight I had a sudden reawakening of that horrible desire . . . had to push him away from me . . . Oh God!*'

Agonized sobbing came from the little recorder. Bruno switched it off.

'What seemed to tip the balance was the accident at the

bullring,' he went on. 'I was out of the way. Her dark side took over and she surrendered completely to the malaise. Her victim was the Gypsy. She must have introduced him to the same sort of experience she had known in Copenhagen, though this time she played the role of seducer. Please understand I don't use that word in quite the normal sense.'

Peter nodded and poured himself another drink from the bottle of Bells.

'Her state was no secret from the Gypsies. Maybe some of them have second sight or ESP or something, but do you remember that hag who read her palm? She must have recognized something. They feared her as an age-old enemy, and once she had corrupted the young Gypsy he became an enemy, too. These people live in a different time-scale from us, they know things we have forgotten.

'The tape does not tell us anything more, but from what I found out the climax came at Les Baux when the Gypsy fell to his death. What was he doing at Les Baux in the first place? People like him are not tourists. I believe he was forced to die.'

'How can you say that?' Peter asked.

'I cannot be sure, but I tell you this: when he fell over that cliff he was impaled on a stake. How strange there should be a stake in that exact spot. It was not part of a fence – there were no other stakes within sight. Strange that the pointed end should be sticking upwards! No, my friend, it has a false ring. I believe he was impaled after he was killed. And you know the significance of that?'

'Certainly.'

'Okay. Let's go back a bit. Stromberg, the name Holly mentions as the stranger she met in Copenhagen, rings the bell, eh? You told me about a Stromberg who visited your hospital and was stabbed ...'

'Hold on, Bruno,' Peter interrupted. 'Stromberg is a common Swedish name.'

'I know, but do you remember I said I'd heard the name before when we were sitting on the beach at Saintes Maries? When I heard Holly's tape diary I remembered she once asked me if I knew anything of a Dr Stromberg, and was he famous? I believe your Stromberg and Holly's are the same person.'

'But I can't believe an eminent neurologist could . . .'

'There are more things in heaven and earth, doctor, than are dreamt of in your philosophy,' Bruno said. 'Listen, I made my enquiries when Holly disappeared. A press card is a great help. I checked at the nearest airport, which is Perpignan. I found from passenger lists that a Dr Stromberg had arrived on a late flight from Paris on the Friday the festival ended. I checked with a car hire firm and found a Dr Stromberg had rented a Mercedes that day. I got them to look up their records, and the doctor returned the car next day. He paid for 480 kilometers, exactly the distance to and from Les Baux.

'Back at the airport I got my friendly, if somewhat greedy, booking clerk to give me the outward passenger lists for Saturday. I found Stromberg had bought an Air France ticket for Helsinki. On the same flight was an English woman by the name of H. Archer.'

Peter looked as if he was going to say something, but Bruno held up his hand.

'Next I did my research into this mysterious Stromberg. Mainly through my Scandinavian contacts I found this. . . .'

Bruno rummaged in his Alitalia bag, produced a black note book and read: 'Stromberg, Axel, and a long list of degrees. Adopted nationality Swedish. Actual nationality unknown. Came from a Red Cross DP camp at the end of the war. Brought up in a home for stateless war orphans in

Stockholm where he was given the name of Stromberg (the place is now closed so I could not get a line on his early life). Brilliant at school, went in for medicine, was considered a genius. Worked for a time in a Swedish hospital, then in the States. While he was there amassed an enormous amount of money. No one knows how, but there are strange theories.'

Peter raised his dark eyebrows in query and Bruno explained he had picked up a hint that Dr Stromberg had been in the 'plasma business'.

'He had been in Haiti during the Duvalier dictatorship when plasma export boomed. Nothing illegal about it, people can sell their blood if they want to. But it is not something a highly respected specialist should be mixed up in. I have no actual proof but it is a straw in the wind.

'Returning to Scandinavia three years ago he obtained permission from the Finnish authorities to build a clinic on the shores of Lake Inari. Said he wanted isolation so he could study extreme cases of psychopathy with the patients under less restraint than was required in populated areas.'

'I know about that,' said Peter. 'He's trying neurological approaches to behaviour rather than psychiatric. If he could come up with an instant cure it would mean relief for hundreds of thousands of people who spend years as psychiatric patients. Some of the new drugs are doing this already, but how effective over a long term . . .'

'Okay, doctor,' interrupted Bruno with a ghost of a smile. 'From the Finnish office of the Global Agency I got information on the clinic. It is built on a peninsula on the east shore of the lake, the nearest settlement being Mustola which is hardly more than a name on the map. The Russian frontier is only a few kilometres away. He also got permission to build an annexe on a small island for his most dangerous patients.'

'Bruno, I can see the case you are building up very clearly,' said Peter. 'But your flair for the sensational is carrying you away. Perhaps Stromberg did have some sexual orgy with Holly in Copenhagen, but that's no crime even for a medical man, provided she was not his patient. Perhaps he did rescue Holly from some trouble in the south of France but that does not make him out to be what you are hinting. In London he behaved perfectly. It was a child who started the bloodthirst business. Stromberg was only a victim of an attack.'

'I'm nearly done,' said Bruno. 'Just answer me this, when Stromberg was stabbed did he lose a lot of blood?'

'There was severe haemorrhage,' admitted Peter. 'He had to have a transfusion.'

'Right,' said Bruno waving his glass excitedly. 'If Stromberg is what I suppose and he lost a lot of blood, what do you think the effect would be – apart from the physical, I mean? He would be desperate for the *essence* which animates him. I believe it was he who stole the blood from the transfusion bottle, and killed the girl when she saw him drinking it.'

Peter said : 'It's too fantastic, Bruno. Look, you know I go along with a lot of this. Because of my theory of contagious blood addiction I was practically kicked out of the London, but what you're trying to make out is too . . .'

'One last point,' Bruno interjected. 'That child patient of yours, what was her name?'

'Britt Hallström.'

'Yes. Where did she have her accident?'

'Her father had taken her on a holiday to Finnmark. I forget the actual name of the place but it was the most northerly town in the world.'

'Hammerfest?'

Peter nodded. Bruno produced a large map of North Europe, and with a blunt finger pointed to the top.

'Look, Peter, there is only one road which runs south from Hammerfest in the whole of that territory. See, it goes past the southern part of Lake Inari. Somewhere near there the Hallström girl had her accident, and was taken to a clinic where she was given blood. Don't you see?'

'Stromberg's clinic?'

'Yes, Stromberg's. Stromberg who induced the blood-thirst in Holly, and who snatched her away when that poor bastard of a Gypsy was dealt with as vampires have been dealt with for centuries; Stromberg who happened to be present when blood was stolen and a girl killed; Stromberg who was probably mixed up in plasma export and has a Haitian negress as his servant. . . .'

He trailed off and the two men sat in a moody silence. Bruno poured more whisky. Peter rubbed his hand wearily over his forehead.

'Okay, Bruno, I'll agree Dr Stromberg could be victim of this vampire contagion.'

Bruno banged the coffee table with the heel of his hand.

'Your theory is the wrong way round,' he almost shouted. 'Because you are a scientific man you think there is some unknown infection which makes people act like old-fashioned vampires. Don't you see it is an old-fashioned vampire who is spreading the infection!

'Damn it, Peter, if a vampire appeared in this modern age what profession would he choose? He could no longer be a count in a Transylvanian castle, slaking his thirst with peasant blood. There is only one profession he could practise and have access to what he wanted without fear of detection.'

Peter gazed at his glass without speaking until Bruno felt impelled to continue.

'With your scientific training it is hard for you to comprehend anything which cannot be written as a formula,' he said. 'You *must* believe in cause and effect, in rational explanation, in protons and neutrons. Yet our whole culture is based on the irrational. Western history was completely altered by the fact a man once rose from the dead which, as a doctor, you know is impossible. Yet, wherever you go in the world, people live lives which – whether they believe in them or not – are still influenced by long ago miracles.'

'The key words there are "long ago",' Peter said.

'Listen, if anyone had told your grandfather when he was a boy that one day he might see moving coloured pictures of men driving a horseless carriage on the moon he would have laughed at them for being crazy. Doesn't it occur to you we may be in the same stage as your grandfather over other things? Might there not be whole areas still to be recognized and comprehended, and that the so-called supernatural could be one of them?'

'I take the point,' Peter said slowly, 'but if Stromberg is a creature of legend, why is he not bound by the laws of legend? Myths say a vampire cannot roam abroad between sunrise and sunset, cannot cross over running water, cannot stand the smell of garlic, and so on.'

'It could be there are laws which reflect belief. Perhaps vampires could not stand garlic in the days when the world believed they hated it. Today they would be released from such restrictions because the belief has faded. It could be equally true of religious miracles. As a Roman Catholic I know there were times when miracles were almost commonplace. That was in the days when people had unshakable credence in them. Now the world is largely atheistic or agnostic there is not the belief to create the ambience for them.'

Peter raised his hands in mock surrender.

'All right, Bruno, you're only underlining what I was already beginning to believe, although I admit I never associated Stromberg with it. Now, what do you want from me?'

'I need you, as a doctor, to get me admitted to Stromberg's clinic.'

'Bruno, I can do better than that,' Peter said and handed him the letter he had earlier shown to Tudor Owens.

The Italian read it with his broad brow wrinkled.

'This I mistrust,' he remarked, handing it back as though the paper itself was contaminated. 'Why should he want you there?'

'Why not? He was very interested in my research at the London. Whatever he is, he is still highly intelligent and no doubt he wants to understand what it is that motivates his kind.'

'But Stromberg would be afraid you would discover too much.'

'I don't think so,' Peter said thoughtfully. 'He only wants me there long enough to set up the research technique, and I'm sure the clinic on the mainland is quite bona fide. It's what he has on his island I should like to see. I'm going to accept the post. The whole thing may turn out to be innocent after all, but I'm going to find out for myself. What strengthens your theory is that he talked Britt Hallström's father into sending her up there. If he is evil, he may have passed the curse on to her by a transfusion of tainted blood after her accident, and now he wants her back.'

'Good Christ!' breathed Bruno. 'I had not thought of that angle.'

'If a doctor wants to be wicked he has the opportunity to be very very wicked.'

'If you accept the post, I am still going too,' declared Bruno. 'You should go normally, but I'll camp secretly near the clinic. You may need a friend on the outside. The weather is good in Lapland at this time of year, and besides I once did a training course with the *Bersaglieri* so I can live happily in the forest for a few weeks.'

167

'I'd be relieved to have a friend at hand,' said Peter. 'I'll cable Stromberg and as soon as I get his reply we'll take the Citroën up to Finland. You can drop me near the clinic and carry on by car. Tomorrow we'll get a detailed map of the area and work out a plan of campaign.'

The thought of positive action was a relief, and both were more relaxed than they had been for days when they finally finished the Bells.

19

Night was left behind as the heavily laden Citroën sped
north along the E4 highway which skirted the Gulf of Both-
nia. Taking turns at the wheel, Peter and Bruno had driven
non-stop since disembarking from the Danish car ferry at
Esjberg. Peter was anxious to arrive according to the sched-
ule set out in a letter from the clinic confirming his appointment and giving instructions for travelling by public trans-
port to Ivalo.

Following the Swedish custom they drove with their lights
on as they followed the road through pleasant farmlands dotted with white, red-roofed houses, belts of dark coniferous
forest and stretches of delicate, pale green birch. Sometimes
they glimpsed the sparkling gulf on their right, and on several occasions had to brake sharply as reindeer, their antlers
thick with velvet, trotted out ahead of them.

They left Sweden at the border town of Haparanda and
crossed the Tornio river into Finland, and a couple of hours
later the road expanded into a wide dual-laned avenue which
was the impressive approach to Rovaniemi, the so-called
capital of Lapland. Its modernity – surrounded by primeval
forest – surprised them. Log cabins would have been more in
keeping than the concrete blocks and brightly painted houses
which had replaced the old town which the German army
had reduced to ashes in 1945.

Bruno glanced at his Rolex watch.

'We made it all right,' he said. 'Over an hour before your bus goes.'

He drove down the Valtakatu, the town's main street, and parked the Citroën beside the bank of the Kemi river. On the opposite side a choir was practising, and their voices floated sweetly across the log-strewn water.

'Before you go to the bus depot let's check the details again,' said Bruno, producing a large-scale map. 'Now, I'm going to camp about here where I should have a good view of the clinic on this peninsula. . . .'

After their plan had been reviewed, Bruno drove to where a large orange bus, with 'Inari' on the front, vibrated gently to its idling engine.

'Good luck, Bruno,' said Peter, lifting out two heavy suit-cases and a canvas rod case. 'I'll make contact tomorrow.'

'*Ciao*, doctor,' Bruno replied and, turning the car, drove northwards.

On the back seat of the bus a Lapp couple, in traditional dress of blue cloth trimmed with red and yellow, spoke softly together. In front sat a dozen English schoolgirls and their Finnish tour leader. At times the young woman read inter-esting facts from a guide book, but their main interest seemed to be giggling and casting wanton glances at Peter as he slumped wearily in his seat.

Soon the bus growled out of Rovaniemi and followed the road which Bruno had already taken. After three miles Peter saw a gallows-shaped signpost on which were the words: 'Napapiiri – Polcirkeln – Arctic Circle – Cercle Polaire'. Good-naturedly the driver stopped to allow the girls to photo-graph each other beneath it with their Instamatics.

Tired from his long journey Peter dozed off and did not awaken until the bus was pulling out of Vuotso some hours later. As he tried to focus his eyes on forest moving past in a deep green blur, he heard the tour leader saying: 'This is the most northerly stage where fir trees can grow and from now on the forest is made up of pine and birch only. Soon we will begin to climb the Raututunturi Mountains which rise to 1625 feet.' The school party giggled afresh at this information and Peter began to feel sympathy for the young guide.

When the bus laboured to the highest point of the range Peter, used to the confines of city life, was awed by the vista. Dark forest rolled to the horizon, dissected by threads of river mirroring the sky which, like all Lapland summer skies, was alive with fast-moving cloud formations.

The tour leader stood up and said in her clipped English as the bus began its downward run to Lake Inari: 'Girls, I will read you about the great lake we approach – "It is not hard to understand how the vast shining sheet of Lake Inari – the largest lake in Lapland and covering 424 square miles – is sacred to the Lapps. Among its three hundred islands is one called Ukonsaari which was vital in their pagan mythology. Here were held sacrifices to their elemental gods. To add an extra note of mystery to the island, ancient Arabian coins have been found there in recent times. The lake lends its name to the largest parish in Finland which covers 5945 square miles, but the population of this huge area is only 1000." '

She closed her book and added: 'The driver tells me there used to be wolves here until the Lapps hunted them to extinction. Now, for no known reason, they have been coming back round the southern shores of the lake. If you go walking in the forest be careful.'

When the bus, its orange paintwork dimmed by clay dust, came to a halt at its destination Peter found himself in a settlement reminiscent of the clapboard townships seen in Western films. The only modern note was a moored seaplane gleaming like a blue dragonfly on the tranquil waters of the lake.

He slung his rod case across his back and took his bags down to the shore where a thirty-foot Fjord cruiser was tied up to a ramshackle jetty. The name *Vlad* was painted in ornate letters on its white transom. Gratefully he put down his cases on the planking and called: 'Ahoy.'

The lithe figure of a negress in a peaked cap and white towelling shirt, which left no doubt as to the tautness of her breasts, appeared from the cabin. She had a narrow jaw and high cheekbones, giving her eyes a slightly oriental slant. Her skin was as black as coal dust.

'You must be Dr Pilgrim,' she said in American-accented English.

'That's right.'

'I'm Saturday. Come aboard and I'll take you to the clinic. There's a road but it's rough even for a jeep.'

Peter lifted his luggage into the cockpit which was already piled with jerrycans of petrol.

'If you smoke go up front,' advised Saturday. 'I've a feeling one of them cans is leaking.'

She settled herself on the helmsman's seat and seconds later a blue haze billowed from the exhausts of the twin Volvo engines. At her command Peter untied the lines and the graceful craft slowly reversed until it was clear of the jetty. Saturday moved the gear into the forward position and steadily opened the throttles. With a subdued roar the Fjord leapt forward, its hull lifted and soon a long wake boiled behind it as it reached its cruising speed of twenty-two knots.

After the drowsy heat of the bus, Peter was exhilarated by the run over the cool water.

'This is a fine craft,' he cried to Saturday.

'Biggest we could get transported in by road,' she answered. 'Makes good time. We'll reach the clinic in three-quarters of an hour.'

Ahead Peter could see a small archipelago of pine-covered

172

islands. They were so low his first impression was of trees growing out of the water. Saturday steered through them without condescending to throttle back. Waves caused by the flying craft washed their shores like miniature rollers.

Past the islands Peter saw another craft, a long, high-prowed Lapp canoe powered by an outboard motor. As the *Vlad* neared it, a blue and red figure stood up in the boat and shook his fist but Saturday ignored the gesture and left the canoe bobbing over her wake.

They passed more islands, some dotted with boulders of red granite, and on one Peter glimpsed a long, windowless building which he guessed was Dr Stromberg's special annexe. Beyond the bows of the Fjord a headland surmounted by a huddle of white buildings began to increase in size.

The many windows reflected the Arctic sun which now hung low over the lake.

Saturday steered to starboard and headed for a pier with the engines still thundering at full throttle. At exactly the right moment she slowed, put the twin screws into reverse to swing the stern in, and the *Vlad* rubbed its fenders against the low wall. The noise of the Volvos brought several people down to the pier. A negro in a dark green tunic took the mooring lines and made the cruiser fast to heavy iron rings.

With a nervous constriction of his throat, Peter saw the tall, white-coated figure of Dr Stromberg stride towards him.

'Welcome, Dr Pilgrim,' he said with a slight smile. 'Welcome to my kingdom.'

Bruno Farina slowed the Citroën and, seeing a suitable clearing, ran it off the dirt road. He turned off the ignition and leaned forward with his face in his hands, overcome with fatigue. After a couple of minutes he straightened, and felt in the pocket of his bush jacket for a crumpled packet of Disque Bleu. He climbed out of the car and kicked pine needles over the marks left by the Michelin tyres on the soft forest floor.

He then took a small axe from the boot and cut branches which he laid against the car to hide its blue metallic paint. He then set out in an easterly direction through the trees, a compass in his hand. After walking over the springy reindeer moss for ten minutes he saw the sparkle of water between the papery trunks of silver birches. He cautiously stepped forward in the shadow of red granite rocks and looked across a bay of blue water to a headland on which stood cube-like buildings.

Congratulating himself on his map-reading, he looked about for a camping site. Between the rocks and first rank of forest trees was a small space completely hidden from the lake, where it would be ideal to pitch his tent.

He returned to the car and unloaded his equipment. Although the sun was low, the exertion of humping it to the lakeside covered his face with sweat which attracted a maddening swarm of midges. He rested briefly before erecting a small green pup tent in which he laid his sleeping bag on an air mattress. Over this he carefully suspended a mosquito net.

Next he unstrapped a couple of large canvas cases containing the components of a collapsible canoe large enough to hold two people. As he struggled to fit this together he heard the sound of distant engines, and peering round the shoulder of rock saw a white cruiser tracing a line of foam towards the headland. Guessing Peter was aboard he gave it an ironical thumbs-up sign and returned to bolting the canoe's struts together. When the slender craft was ready for service he hid it in a patch of undergrowth.

By now the sun was almost touching the horizon, the lowest it would go in this latitude, and checking his watch Bruno realized it was midnight. He brought out a jar of Nescafe, lit a smokeless butane camping stove and was soon sitting with

174

his back against the warm granite and a steaming mug in his hand. He was so tired his head nodded and it was the pain of the hot drink spilling on to his leg which woke him.

He crawled into the tent and thankfully sank on the air mattress. From a long distance away there came a strange yelping and his hand felt for the reassurance of the high-velocity Hornet .22 rifle which had been brought from London under the rear seat of the Citroën. He wished it was a heavier calibre weapon, but this was the only type he had been able to buy.

After waking and shaving with a battery razor, Bruno unpacked his Pentax to which he attached a massive telephoto lens. This he mounted on a heavy duty tripod and set up in the shadow of the rock, aimed at the clinic buildings. By looking through the reflex viewfinder, he could observe them as well as if he had binoculars. Tiny figures walked on terraces surrounding the clinic. He noticed a pencil line of smoke rising from the tall chimney of a building some distance from the main block. He surmised this was the power house where diesel-driven generators provided electricity for Dr Stromberg's community.

Having taken several photographs, he left the equipment as it was and went through the forest to make sure the car was still safely hidden. As a precaution he carried the .22. After this the only break in the monotony was when he cooked himself a meal.

He read and dozed through the bright day until the sun approached its nadir and he unpacked a small Hitachi two-way radio purchased from a Tottenham Court Road hifi shop. He connected it by a lead to the pocket tape recorder on which he had played Holly's taped diary and extended the telescopic aerial. Looking at his watch, he saw it was five minutes to midnight. The set hummed slightly as he switched on.

The sun threw a long, blood-streaked reflection across the glassy lake, and the tranquillity of the scene affected the Italian's quick imagination – he began to sense that the still timber about him was alive. He knew it would be ridiculous to think a tree had a soul, but perhaps such a vast multitude could have a collective entity. . . .

His musing was interrupted exactly at twelve o'clock by Peter's voice whispering from the walkie-talkie: 'Hello, Bruno. Hello, Bruno. Can you hear me?'

Bruno held the device up to his mouth and answered: 'Bruno here. This thing works fine. I've got it hooked up to the tape to keep a record.'

'Good. The fishing gear provided an excuse for leaving the clinic. I'm in a cove on the lakeshore, but I've got the rod out just in case anyone comes along. Are you set up all right?'

'Sure, but I heard a damn wolf last night. What has been happening at the clinic?'

'I was brought over here in Stromberg's power cruiser, the *Vlad*, with a sexy-looking Haitian girl at the wheel by name of Saturday. Stromberg also has three Haitian men as general factotums.'

'I heard a whisper about them when I was researching the doctor. In the heyday of Papa Doc on Haiti they were all Tontons Macoutes – including the girl.'

'What?'

'The Tonton Macoute was Papa Doc's secret police. The Haitians believed that Papa was a voodoo high priest as well as dictator, and some of the Tontons were his zombies. You know, animated corpses. It's appropriate the girl should call herself Saturday because the voodoo God of the Graveyard is Baron Samedi. Have you found any trace of Holly?'

'Not a thing, but if she's up here I'll bet she's out on that island. The clinic is all above board. There are about twenty patients and each has a private room complete with a concealed infra-red TV surveillance system. Most of the staff don't speak English, but I've been working with a nurse who can translate for me. Apart from Britt, there are two other narcoleptics here and I've been busy setting up behaviour-recording systems. Britt woke briefly but I don't think she recognized me. No sign of the bloodthirst in her today.

'In fact, Bruno, if the World Health Organization sent an investigating team here they'd only find things to praise. Most of the patients are in psychosis, but they are very well cared for. There's plenty of well-trained staff, and they have great respect for Stromberg.'

As Bruno gazed at the small box from which Peter's voice hissed there was a look of disappointment on his face.

'Having said all that,' it continued, 'I must tell you I be-lieve you're right. I just sense there's something evil here! I'm sure the answer is on the island. I questioned Stromberg about it, but he just said there were dangerous patients there but they didn't come within my scope.

'I'd better get back to my fishing now. If I can catch some-thing it'll strengthen my alibi. I said I was going angling because, not being used to twenty-four hours of daylight, I couldn't sleep.'

Slowly Bruno telescoped the aerial and put the radio and the tiny recorder into the pockets of his jacket. He felt lonely and in the distance he heard the cry of a wolf.

20

It seemed to Peter he had only closed his eyes when the distant rumble of the *Vlad*'s twin engines roused him. Disorientated by Lapland's nightless summer days he got a shock when he glanced at his watch. Still only half awake, he reached for his clothes, scattered about the room which was furnished in the impersonal style of a modern hotel, with bleached wood furniture and neutral wall colours.

A few minutes later he was alone in the staff dining room, breakfasting on black coffee and the usual smörgaasbord.

'Good morning, Dr Pilgrim.'

Peter looked up and saw Dr Stromberg looming above him. As usual he was immaculately groomed with his glossy hair curling carefully over his brow, though no matter how closely he shaved the bristles beneath his pallid skin gave it a dark tinge.

'You will find the continuous daylight upsetting at first,' he said, 'but do not worry, you will soon be acclimatized. The winter night is more difficult; then people sometimes get the "black sickness" which can only be cured by going south where they can see daylight.'

'Really?' Peter said. Now his mind harboured suspicions – and he admitted they were fantastic suspicions – about the neuro-surgeon, he felt uneasy in his presence, almost afraid he could read his thoughts.

'I have very good news,' Stromberg continued. 'You have seen our operating theatre, which has never been put to use.

That can now be rectified, because a fully qualified neurological theatre sister has arrived. Miss Saturday has taken the cruiser to collect her. You may even know her, as she recently qualified at the London Hospital for Diseases of the Nervous System. A French woman by the name of Clair.'

Peter's heart accelerated, but he kept his eyes on his plate.

'Perhaps I'll recognize her when I see her,' he muttered.

'Perhaps. And how are you settling in here?'

'Very well. I hope to start the iontophoretic programme soon,' said Peter. 'Do you want to see any preliminary reports on the Hallström girl and the others?'

'There is no hurry, Dr Pilgrim. I am happy to leave everything connected with that research in your capable hands. Are you having any luck with your fishing?'

'I live in hopes. But the fish don't come in close. I don't suppose you have a small boat I could borrow?'

'Regrettably, no,' Stromberg said with a slight smile on his full lips. 'The *Vlad* is the only craft we have here. To be frank with you, I have no wish for any of our walking patients attempting to row over to the annexe. That is what you call, out of bounds.'

'I understand,' said Peter. 'Now if you will excuse me . . . nurse will be waiting for me to start today's tests.'

'Certainly, doctor. If you find there is extra apparatus you require, please let me know within the next two days. After that I have to spend a week in Helsinki at a conference.'

Peter nodded and walked down a spacious corridor to the suite where his subjects were sleeping peacefully. He spoke into a wall microphone connected to a room which appeared like the control centre of a television studio. Racks of monitors showed a controller the well-lit interiors of the patients' rooms. Some bed-ridden patients had electronic sensors taped to their bodies so heart-beat, temperature and respiration appeared as rhythmic patterns on green oscilloscope screens.

When Peter's voice issued from a loudspeaker, the controller pressed one of a score of illuminated keys on his console and the door to Britt's room slid open electrically. As most of the patients were potentially dangerous, the doors were without conventional handles.

Nurse Bergman was sitting beside the bed, reading a story to Britt who was in one of her rare periods of wakefulness.

'Good morning, doctor,' said the nurse. 'Our little patient is awake, so I am reading her the story of the Little Snow Princess. I told her she is like a snow princess herself.'

Peter agreed. The sunlight flooding through the hermetically sealed window shone on Britt's silver blonde hair and her delicate nordic features. It was hard to imagine such a child was capable of sinking her teeth into a man's throat.

'Please continue,' Peter said. 'I'd hate to interrupt. I'll go through these graphs, and when you are ready we'll start the phased electromyograms.' While nurse continued the tale in Swedish and Britt held a troll doll, Peter was grateful for time to think. He sank into an inflated plastic chair and, as he pretended to study a sheaf of papers, let his mind digest Stromberg's words.

Anne-Marie was on her way to the clinic!

At first it seemed incredible, but as he thought about it the more logical it became. Stromberg needed theatre staff now his clinic was fully operational, and no doubt he had contacted Anne-Marie through the London. Her course was over, she needed a job and perhaps Scandinavia had appealed more than Paris. He wondered if she had broken with her husband?

Could she have known he was here?

A sinister suspicion entered his mind. Had Stromberg guessed of his relationship with Anne-Marie and decided to get them both to Inari because of the conjectures he held over the behaviour of Britt and Lionel Tedworth in London?

(Holly might have told Stromberg of their so-called love affair.)

That's ridiculous, he told himself. I only became suspicious of Stromberg after Bruno called on me in London. There is nothing to connect Anne-Marie with that. But . . .

'Dr Pilgrim.' Nurse Bergman's clipped accent broke his train of thought. 'The little girl has gone back to sleep. We can start the tests whenever you like.'

'Right,' Peter said. 'Did it end happily?'

'Pardon me?'

'The story. Did the Snow Princess escape from the Wolf King?'

'There are still many pages to read. And please do not talk of wolves.' She gave a mock shudder. 'They say the wolves are returning to the forest. It must be so because I have seen one of the black men with a gun.'

Lunch had just concluded when the *Vlad* neatly sidled up to the clinic pier. From a terrace Peter saw Anne-Marie, a slender figure in silver-grey slacks and fawn windcheater, disembark while one of Stromberg's Haitian servants hefted her suitcases from the cockpit. As he watched Stromberg greet her with a formal bow, he realized that, despite the mental agony he had suffered over her mysterious husband, he still loved her as much as ever.

When the French girl had refreshed herself after the journey, she was ushered into the common-room whose landscape windows presented a panorama of the island-dotted lake. Her eyes widened as she saw Peter, but he pretended not to notice and lowered his eyes to a month-old copy of *The Lancet*. Dr Stromberg made the introductions.

'. . . this is Dr Hansen, my second in command . . . and this is Dr Pilgrim whom you may have seen at the London. Mademoiselle Clair – Dr Pilgrim.'

Peter stood up and said: 'Ah yes, the London eh? Pleased

to meet you. Excuse me, I have some tests under way.' And he made a quick exit. Thank God she had not cried out with surprise at seeing him, he thought as he strode down the corridor of handleless doors. He wanted to be alone with her when it was the time for explanations.

It was ten o'clock in the bright evening as Peter sat with his back against a rock and his fishing rod angled over the quiet water. A small bank covered with dwarf birch hid the clinic from view. Occasionally the breeze carried faint cries from some members of the staff who, with their day's duty over, were relaxing on the clinic's tennis court.

'Peter!' Anne-Marie stood by the bank, looking down on him.

'Hello, Anne-Marie,' he answered, his eyes fixed on the red float bobbing in front of him.

'Peter, did you arrange for Dr Stromberg to offer me this job?'

'Honestly, I was as surprised to see you as you were to see me.'

'Is that true?'

'Yes. But in one way I'm glad you're here.'

'Oh?'

'Yes.' He moved the rod slightly to make the float dance to another spot. 'I apologize for hitting you at the *Maison*. It was inexcusable, and I regret it more than ...'

'Peter!'

'Yes?'

'Peter-Pierre, kiss me.'

He looked up at last. The low sun gave a warm lustre to the pale gold hair which fell across her face. Next moment he was holding her in his arms.

When they released each other she sat beside him while he squinted at the float.

182

'I didn't know your Paris address so I couldn't write,' he said.

'My letter is probably waiting for you in London. I wrote care of the hospital.'

'What did you say?'

'Only that my father gave Alain the finance he wanted for his wretched gallery, in return for agreeing to get the divorce through quickly. It was over long ago, Peter. What I felt for him was killed within months of the wedding.'

'Tell me some other time,' said Peter. 'I don't want to talk about it now. You do love me, don't you?'

'If ever I had any doubts, I was sure of it when you drove off so dramatically.'

He grinned. 'That makes two of us.'

'What a wonderful coincidence for us to meet here.'

'I hope it's a coincidence.'

'What do you mean?'

Then he told her in great detail how Bruno had arrived in London with Holly's taped diary.

'That's why I gave you the cold shoulder when you arrived,' he explained. 'I didn't want Stromberg to see any connection between us. I don't want you to get involved. . . .'

'Peter, I am involved because you are. Poor Holly. I had no idea . . . and you think she may be out on that island?'

He nodded.

'But, Peter, this is so like a Poe story – I cannot believe it.'

He glanced at his watch.

'This should prove we mean business,' he said and brought out the little radio. 'Hello, Bruno. Hello, Bruno.'

A quiet answer came from the microphone-speaker: 'Hearing you clear, doctor.'

He handed the instrument to Anne-Marie and winked at her.

'Is that Bruno Farina?' whispered Anne-Marie.

'Who the hell is that?'

Peter took the Hitachi back and quickly explained. Then he said: 'Listen, Bruno, this is important. Stromberg is leaving for Helsinki the day after tomorrow. This gives me a chance to get to the island. There are no boats here, apart from the *Vlad*, so I'll use the canoe. Dismantle and take it through the forest to the inlet where that pine stands by itself. Hide it in the reeds under the tree. Okay?'

'It took me an hour to put it together, now I have to take it apart again,' Bruno's metallic voice complained. 'Why can't I paddle across?'

Peter explained he wanted him to remain at large so he could act in case of an emergency.

'At least, I'm officially one of the staff there,' he continued. 'If the Tontons get suspicious I can point out I'm crazy about fishing. If they caught you they could drown you in the lake and no one'd be the wiser.'

'All right, but be careful.'

'You bet I'll be careful. I'll take the transceiver with me, and you open the channel every hour on the hour in case I have anything to report.'

'Okay. Give Anne-Marie a kiss for me.'

Peter switched off.

'Now, darling, you'd better go back and get some sleep. I'll stay here for another half hour and try to get a bite. I don't want them to realize you've been with me.'

They kissed and she disappeared into the rustling silver birches which lined the lake margin.

21

With a clipboard of notes in his hand, Peter Pilgrim walked down a long passage where circular windows overlooked Lake Inari. A sudden rainstorm had blown up and large drops streamed down the plate glass, distorting the lake, which had turned a dirty grey, and the threshing trees lining it. Peter wondered how Bruno was making out in his small tent.

But he forgot his friend when he saw Anne-Marie walking towards him in a white terylene uniform with her nursing medals and fob watch hanging from the top pocket. As she drew nearer he could see her face was white and strained.

'Peter, I must talk to you,' she said as they met.

'Are you all right, Anne-Marie?'

She nodded. 'Where can we meet so it will seem natural?'

'The rain's nearly over. Let's meet at the tennis court at lunch break. That'll seem innocent enough.'

'All right. *Sacré Coeur*, I'll be glad when we're away from here.'

Wraiths of steam were rising from the asphalt court when Peter sauntered out at midday. The rain clouds had been blown away and now the sun made the air humid. He stood with a knot of staff members, watching Nurse Bergman exchanging shots with plump Dr Hansen. In the background a Haitian polished Dr Stromberg's black Mercedes. The doors gaped and Peter glimpsed the wolfskin seat covers Holly had mentioned on her tape.

'Hello, Dr Pilgrim,' Anne-Marie said casually. 'Isn't it warm?'

'Hello, Sister Clair,' he answered politely. 'It gets surprisingly hot in these northern latitudes. The thermometer sometimes goes up to ninety degrees.'

'Really? Shall we sit down and wait for the court to be free?'

'Splendid.'

They walked to a bench out of earshot of the others.

'Anne-Marie, what's the matter? You looked very strained this morning.'

'Oh, Peter, it was dreadful. Something horrible happened in the night. I had pulled the blind down to make it dark and I dozed off. Then I had a very vivid dream.'

She coloured slightly.

'To be honest, I dreamed you were in bed with me and we were making love. It was so real. I could feel your hands touching me, and particularly I was aware of your mouth on my skin.'

'Go on,' said Peter. 'This is fascinating – I wish I'd been there in the flesh.'

'You will be soon, I hope,' she smiled. 'I don't suppose an erotic dream is unusual. Most people have them, and I had been thinking about you when I went to sleep. But this one was almost too vivid for a dream; your mouth felt so real I began to wake up.

'It was very strange. I was in that funny state between waking and sleeping, just drifting and enjoying the sensation . . . for a moment I thought you'd risked the TV cameras and come to me. Then I woke up properly and, Peter, I wasn't alone.'

'What?'

'Yes. I felt this body in the bed. Its arms were round me and its mouth was . . . was at my breast. I switched on the bedside lamp and I saw it was Britt Hallström.'

'My God!'

'I was terrified because of what she did to that orderly. I touched my throat to see if it was bleeding, but she had not bitten me there. She was just using me like a lover. . . .'

She rubbed her hand across her violet eyes.

'At least I know now I haven't any lesbian tendencies,' she said with a shaky laugh. 'At least, not with little girls.'

'What happened then?'

'It was grotesque. I tried to push her away, but she just whispered to me in Swedish. I couldn't understand the words, but I got the message. When she saw I wasn't interested in . . . well, you know . . . she spat at me and ran out of the door. Afterwards I might have thought it was a nightmare, except for her nightgown on the floor, and a certain soreness.'

'Anne-Marie, you know what this means?'

'I think so. The doors of the patients' room can only be worked by remote control. Someone deliberately opened the door of Britt's room for her to find her way to mine . . . to make me one of them.'

She lowered her head and Peter saw tears gathering in her eyes.

'That's it, all right,' Peter agreed. 'Thank God you woke up before she . . . before she . . .' He trailed off, not wishing to put his thoughts into words.

'Peter, we must get out of here.'

He nodded. 'I'm going to take a look at that island, then we'll meet up with Bruno and get the Citroën.'

'I'm coming with you in the canoe.'

'Yes, we must keep together. Stromberg will be leaving this afternoon. Once the *Vlad* gets clear we'll cross to the island. You won't have to spend another night here.'

From the tennis court Nurse Bergman called to them:

'We have finished. You can play now.'

'We'd better keep up the pretence,' said Peter, and the two young people strolled out to play as though they had not a care in the world.

Bruno Farina lay on his back close to the tent and watched tatters of cirrus move slowly across the sky. He had just concluded a brief radio conversation with Peter who reported that Stromberg had left with Saturday and two of his black servants in the *Vlad*. When the sun was lower he and Anne-Marie would set out for the island in the canoe.

When Bruno asked why Anne-Marie was taking the risk, Peter said: 'She refuses to be left behind. Besides, I think she'll be safer with me after what happened last night.'

'Good luck to you both then,' Bruno had said. 'I'll listen out for you on the hour. *Ciao!*'

As usual he felt lonely when the tenuous link ended. But he was not as alone as he thought; in the deep shadow of the trees a stocky man with a broad flat face was watching him with the unflickering gaze of a patient hunter.

Peter Pilgrim and Anne-Marie slipped away from the clinic while the staff were busy with the evening meals. They quickly crossed the tennis court, where earlier the French girl had managed to beat Peter despite her succuba experience, and hand-in-hand ran through the forest, keeping the lake to their left.

Breathlessly they reached the inlet where a tall pine stood like a lonely sentinel. It took them several minutes to locate the canoe which Bruno had camouflaged so thoroughly. Careful not to tear its fabric against the rocks, Peter launched it.

'Ever done any canoeing?' he asked.

She shook her head. 'But don't worry, I can swim like a fish if we tip over.'

'We won't tip if you sit still amidships. Luckily my father used to take me canoeing when I was a boy.'

After Anne-Marie had settled herself, he pushed the frail craft forward and adroitly climbed in. He used the single-bladed paddle Indian-style, and found he still had enough skill not to have to cross it from side to side. For a while he skirted the shore to keep out of sight of the clinic, then turned and headed in the direction of the pine-covered islands. In the distance the orange light of the low sun flashed on the clinic windows, and he prayed they would not be spotted by the remaining Tonton Macoute while they crossed the open water.

Paddling so hard trickles of sweat ran into his eyes, Peter soon reached the cover of the first island. He slowed to get his breath, then steered towards the island on which he had seen the square windowless building. It was higher than the others in the group, with massive granite boulders tumbled on its shores.

He dug the paddle into the water and expertly drove the canoe's bows up a tiny beach of dark sand. Anne-Marie jumped ashore and helped Peter run the craft out of the water.

'The annexe is on the other side,' he told her. 'I'll contact Bruno to tell him we've arrived safely, then we'll cross over.'

They sat in the shade of a lichened monolith. While Peter extended the aerial, Anne-Marie pointed to the surface of the stone. On it was carved concentric rings and spirals through which ran a snake-like line.

'Must be an ancient Lapp monument,' he commented. 'Hello . . . Hello . . . Bruno? We've made it. We're going to investigate now. Wish us luck!'

189

It took only a few minutes to walk through the pines to where the tall rectangular building stood. A smaller one stood nearby built of concrete blocks, from which came the faint thump-thump of a diesel generator. Behind this was a large fuel storage tank.

'There's the entrance,' whispered Anne-Marie, pointing to a wide arched door.

She added with a slight shiver: 'It's more like the door of a tomb.'

Peter nodded agreement, and without another word they softly approached the anonymous building. On the lintel above the bronzed portal was carved in Gothic lettering: *Et ego in Arcadia.*

'Seems a damn strange hospital annexe,' muttered Peter. He pressed his hands on the door and it slowly creaked inward.

'Wish us luck!' came the distorted voice from Bruno's transceiver.

' "Luck," ' muttered Bruno as he switched it off and ran the aerial into the socket. He looked up to see a silent circle of impassive men surrounding his small camp, each dressed in a baggy blue costume with red and yellow fringes. On their feet were soft boots of reindeer hide and in their hands rifles pointed steadily at him.

Only one was not in Lapp costume, a broad, middle-aged man who wore a black leather flying jacket. There was a look of lively intelligence on his wide features. His brown hair was streaked with blond where sun and wind had bleached out the colour.

'I think English is our common language,' he said to the tensed Italian.

Bruno nodded.

'Good,' said the man, squatting near the rock against

190

which Bruno was sitting. 'My name is Uutsi, and I am what you might call the captain round here – is that the word? It is quite a few years since I studied English at Uppsala University.'

'It'll do,' said Bruno. 'And who are these gentlemen with the firearms?' From his pocket he took a white packet of Disque Bleu, tore it open and proffered it to Uutsi.

'Thank you,' he said, taking a cigarette. 'As you can see, we are Sabme – what the Finns call Lapps, which simply means "Land's end folk".'

Bruno nodded.

'At the moment we are on a wolf hunt.'

'I have heard wolves,' Bruno remarked tossing the packet to the nearest Lapp. The man caught it with his free hand, but his eyes never left the Italian.

'We are after a very big wolf,' said Uutsi.

'So am I,' said Bruno. He indicated his camera mounted on the tripod. 'But I use different weapons.'

'I know,' said Uutsi. 'I have picked up several of your walkie-talkie transmissions.'

Bruno exhaled but said nothing. As yet he was not sure whether this strange band was friend or foe. Was he the 'big wolf', or was it someone else? Looking at their determined, slightly Asian features he hoped he was not the wolf.

'Time passes, so I must be brief and frank,' continued Uutsi. 'I picked up your talk on the radio in my aircraft. I have a floatplane moored at Ivalo. So I sent one of my men to watch you. It was mainly for your own protection. There are evil people abroad.'

Bruno's surprise must have shown in his face.

'You are surprised I have a plane,' laughed Uutsi. 'Then you do not understand us Sabme. Because we prefer our old costumes and follow our reindeer as we have done for centuries, it does not mean we scorn the advantages of the twentieth century. Thanks to our great herds we are not a poor folk, but we have not changed our basic way of life because it is the life we want. We are a very old people, and we live in exactly the same territory as we did when we were first mentioned in recorded history. Few races can claim that.

'And because we are an old people in an old land, the forests, lakes and even the rocks have a mystical significance for us. This land is in our blood, which is why we do not migrate south to the cities.'

'I can understand that,' said Bruno. 'It's just that I didn't consider the floatplane.'

'It's the only way of quick travel here,' Uutsi explained. 'There are always lakes to land on, and as headman I travel far afield in the summer when my people are following the herds north. It is useful in case of emergency, too. In winter I have skis fitted.'

The Lapp turned and spoke to his men who lowered their rifles and sat down, smoking Bruno's cigarettes.

'This lake of Inari is our most sacred place,' Uutsi continued in English. 'To us it is as important as Mecca to a Moslem or Jerusalem to a Jew. Out there is an island which has been in our folklore since our folklore began. In the old days the Midwinter Sacrifice was made there to call back the summer. Today our most sacred things – what is the word, totems? – are kept there. There are ancient graves and even treasures of gold. No Sabme would dare desecrate such a sacred place.'

'I understand,' Bruno said. 'But I swear to you that we had no thought of plundering your holy places.'

'Of that I am sure,' said Uutsi. 'If you had, you might have been sacrificed even though we have been Christianized since the eighteenth century – to some extent at least. When one of our wise old men uses his drum to read the future there is a symbol of the Virgin Mary painted on the skin as well as the crossed hammers of Thor.'

He paused and looked sideways across the gleaming expanse of lake.

'But there has been desecration,' he continued softly. 'One has come and put his own temple on our island. We do not object to the hospital on the mainland, for we recognize progress; what we cannot allow is a stranger setting up his shrine over the graves of our ancestors.'

'You mean Dr Stromberg's building on the island?'

Uutsi inclined his head.

'From listening to the talk between you and the man you call "doctor", I believe you are after the same big wolf. Our wisemen sense nothing but evil in him. They say he does not have a spirit like other men. That is the talk of old men, but, as I told you, we are a very old people and our memories are long.

'Whether or not he is what they say does not concern me. My duty is to protect our holy place. Please explain exactly your interest, for I did not understand everything from the radio.'

'It is simple,' Bruno said. 'My friend and I believe this man, who has built on your island, is an evil one who has stolen a woman who means much to me. What he has on his island we do not know, but we have come a long way to find out. At this moment my friend is out there.'

Uutsi spoke to his followers. They climbed to their feet and picked up their rifles.

'Your camera looks expensive. You had better pack it up,' said the headman. 'You are coming with us on our wolf hunt.'

Quickly Bruno unscrewed the telephoto lens from the Pentax and put it away in his camera bag.

'It is strange,' mused Uutsi as he waited for him. 'Since that one came to Inari the wolves have been assembling – the oldest enemy of the Sabme. It is a bad omen. Come.' And Bruno followed the silent Lapps into the forest.

22

The portal opened and Peter and Anne-Marie stepped into a bare antechamber with two doors. One opened into a corridor similar to those in the main clinic with the same pastel walls. The only difference was the absence of windows, the illumination coming from fluorescent tubes.

'Good God!' he exclaimed as he passed through the other doorway. 'Have you ever seen anything like this!'

Anne-Marie followed him down some steps into the body of a high, vaulted hall. It was lit by coloured rays of light streaming through windows of exquisite stained glass. It was an extraordinary replica of the type of mediaeval church built into a castle for the use of the baron and his retainers. The floor beneath their feet was made of massive flagstones, the walls were of rough-hewn blocks. In the centre was a black-draped catafalque on which rested an ornately carved coffin of oak. It was open.

With a sense of dread Peter and Anne-Marie approached it. Splashes of colour reflected on its highly polished surfaces from one of the lancet windows. Cautiously they looked over the side, but all that met their eyes was a padded lining of scarlet silk.

'Peter,' said Anne-Marie. 'What can this be?'

'I don't know who the casket is for, but I suppose you could logically say this is the clinic's chapel,' he answered in a whisper. 'But it seems too ancient – it almost smells ancient. Look at those heraldic shields hanging on the pillars.'

'When we saw the outside of the building there were no windows,' Anne-Marie said. 'Yet there's sunlight coming through the stained glass.'

Peter looked up at the multi-hued panes whose leaded shapes seemed to represent allegorical figures. Above the marble altar at the far end a huge window portrayed the Raising of Lazarus in glowing colours.

'There must be special lighting behind the glass,' he said. 'But the effect is stunning.'

They walked softly to the altar. Instead of the conventional cross, it had a large upright block of transparent acrylic in which was embedded something shining silver.

'I think we ought to get out,' murmured Anne-Marie with a shudder. To Peter's surprise she crossed herself.

'Remember I'm a staff doctor looking over the clinic's amenities,' he said reassuringly as he stepped up to the altar and gazed into the crystalline cube.

'What is it?' Anne-Marie asked, peering over his shoulder.

'It's an old silver plate,' he answered. 'There's a hole in each corner where it's been screwed on to something. It's like the plates they used to fix on to coffin lids. There's writing engraved on it.'

Together they read: 'Janos Nádasdy + 1704–1714 + Requiescat in pace.'

'Nádasdy – Nádasdy,' murmured Anne-Marie, 'I have heard that name before.'

'My God, so have I!' exclaimed Peter. 'Do you remember my father telling us about the Hungarian Countess Elizabeth Bathori who killed over six hundred girls for their blood? That was her maiden name. She was married to a Count Nádasdy and had four children. This must be the coffin inscription for a descendant of the Countess.'

'He was only a child when he died.'

'*If* he died.'

196

'Peter, you can't mean that Stromberg . . .'

He shrugged.

'Come on, we must search. Look, there's a door to the left of the altar.'

Nervously they approached the arched doorway which was hung with a black velvet curtain. Peter drew it to one side and saw a spiral staircase leading downwards. White light reflected on the stone wall and, with his left hand holding the newel, he descended. Anne-Marie followed behind in his grotesque shadow. At the bottom they found they had entered the crypt of the chapel, but there was no resemblance to its antique atmosphere.

Thick rugs covered the floor, the temperature was kept too warm by means of electric oil-filled radiators, the bright light shone from fluorescent tubes while incongruously a tall chromium transfusion stand stood in a corner. In another was a purring refrigerator. There were easy chairs, a low table with books on it, and against the far wall a day bed covered with a rug made from animal skins.

It was what lay on the rug which held the incredulous gaze of Peter and Anne-Marie – a thin, waxy-faced figure wrapped in a loose robe of some black material. There was a metal bracelet on its wrist, from which hung a thin iron chain. It coiled across the rugs to where its last link was locked to a great staple set in the wall. Only the rich auburn hair framing the skeletal face of the prisoner told them they had found Holly Archer.

In fascinated horror Anne-Marie and Peter watched the creature which was once their friend turn her lack-lustre eyes upon them.

'Why have you come here?' she asked in a slow, strangely mechanical voice. 'Only Janos comes here.'

She moved her arm and the chain rattled.

'Once I thought love was enough to bind me, but he changed it into a bond of iron.'

'Holly, Holly darling,' sighed Anne-Marie. 'We have come to take you away. Bruno is not far away. You remember Bruno Farina?'

The thing on the bed slowly sat up and, reaching to the low table, picked up a box of black cigarettes. She lit one with the blue Stick lighter Bruno had given her at Saintes Maries de la Mer and slowly exhaled, her livid lips a grimace of satisfaction.

'I smoke and wait for Janos,' she said. 'And while I wait I have such dreams.'

'A complete personality change,' Peter muttered to Anne-Marie. 'Listen, Holly, who is Janos? Is he the tall doctor who you met in Copenhagen?'

'Janos came for me when the Gypsy flew over the cliff,' she said. 'Like a bird he went, out out over the plain. There was danger, and then there was Janos and no more fear. Such pleasure, and such dreams! But now I stay here because Janos knows I have learned to hate.' There was a long silence.

'Why do you hate?' asked Peter. 'Is it Janos you hate?'

She looked up with sorrowful lunatic eyes.

'Janos I hate because my love means nothing to him now. He is old . . . old. His love was lost long ago. A little girl with silver-gold hair, he said, who wept beside his bed. He has found her again, but she is not me, not me!'

'Who has he found, Holly?' whispered Peter.

'His dream bride. He has found her again . . . the same face, the same hair. Now he only waits for her to become a woman, then I shall be . . .'

She waved her hand vaguely and the cigarette left a scrawl of smoke.

'I shall be lost in my dream for ever,' she continued at last.

'That is why I hate him. My love he had, my body was his, yet that was not enough – I am not his child love, I am not Britt.'

'Britt!' gasped Anne-Marie. 'Peter, take me from here. I'm going mad!'

'Hold on, darling,' he said. 'We've got to help her.'

'This time her name is Britt, a child of the cold sun,' Holly went on in her dead voice. 'She will be his bride, yet still he comes to me. . . .'

Anne-Marie turned away, her hand clasped tightly across her mouth to stifle the scream which was growing in her throat. Peter tugged with all his strength at the chain, but the staple in the wall was immovable.

'We must get away,' Anne-Marie whimpered. 'She is lost and crazy. There is nothing we can do. We must save ourselves.'

'You cannot unlock me,' Holly said. 'Janos would not dare have me free. He knows what I should do if I had the chance. I have strange power and I would destroy him.'

Her eyelids began to flicker. She dropped the cigarette into an ashtray and lay back on the furs exhausted. Peter saw dark marks where transfusion needles had entered her veins.

Suddenly she sat up.

'Have I seen you before? Why are you here? Does Janos know?'

'Crazy!' sobbed Anne-Marie. 'Her mind has gone.'

'We must go outside so I can call Bruno,' Peter said. 'We can't abandon her to him.'

'It is too late,' wailed Anne-Marie. 'But come!'

Frantically she climbed the steps and burst through the black curtain into the chapel, then stopped and leaned against the cold altar for support.

In the centre of the nave, close to the open coffin, stood Stromberg, ominous in a black silk sweater and black slacks.

At the far end by the door lounged his two bodyguards. Their teeth showed brilliant white in water-melon grins.

'You have entered a forbidden realm,' he said softly, 'but I expected it, Dr Pilgrim. For a long time I have recognized you as a danger. And you, Mademoiselle Clair. By pretending to go away, I have proved my suspicions.

'At the hospital in London I knew from your notes you saw deeply into the case of the child Britt. May I pay you the compliment of saying you are too imaginative to be a man of science, though, of course, you tried to find an answer through science. When Sir Henry discussed it with me, we both agreed you had gone too far with your theories based on the tales of old wives.' He laughed gently. 'Fate marked you, doctor, when the fool who is Britt's father flew her to London.'

Peter clasped Anne-Marie's hand to give her courage and said evenly: 'Tell me, Dr Stromberg, did you pass the contagion on to her?'

'With my own blood . . . a bond was made that unites us irrevocably,' he answered sombrely. 'In this you and your kind can only see evil, for you are the children of Eve while my kind are the children of Lilith.'

He paused, walked to the altar and pointed to the silver plate suspended in its transparent reliquary.

'Yet one thing we have in common, the need for identity,' he went on. 'Can you imagine, doctor, the experience of waking as a child in an alien world, bewildered by vague memory, mourning for a love long lost and possessed by a thirst it would be death to reveal? I knew not who I was; I knew not *what* I was!

'But I was endowed with the intelligence of my line. I observed and schemed and studied; studied to gain knowledge of my condition and to earn power enough to satisfy my need. You know how successful I have been. Yet the mystery of my origin remained. I searched Europe for that small piece of metal you see there, and when I found it in a dismal room in London it told me all I needed to know. Though I suffered a wound in getting it which could have endangered my grand design, it identified me.'

He waved his white well-groomed hand round the chapel, its gloom cut by slanting rays of tinted light.

'This grew from childish impressions which survived from the old time. A re-created environment where once I knew joy.'

'And the coffin?' Peter asked.

'As you have observed, doctor, my kind can be vulnerable to cataleptic trance. With knowledge I have gained I can predict when this is going to happen to me, and it is my fancy to rest as my ancestors rest.'

There was silence in the seemingly ancient chapel.

'And what about Hol . . . your prisoner in the crypt?' Anne-Marie demanded bravely.

'She was a willing victim, mademoiselle. Blood calls to blood, and as your Bible says the life of all flesh is the blood thereof. What greater token of love can she give me than to grant the essence vital to my continuation!'

Stromberg shifted his eyes from the coffin plate which had such significance for him, and looked directly at Peter. 'Of course, doctor, I cannot allow you to leave with this knowledge in your mind.'

'It would be impossible to expect you to have a conscience over murder when you can corrupt children with your own tainted blood,' Peter retorted. 'But I warn you if you or your Tonton thugs kill me, there will be enough evidence to send you to your own particular hell.'

Stromberg's fleshy lips tightened into a mirthless smile.

'Dr Pilgrim, how can you suggest such a thing? Nothing so crude had entered my head. No, you will be returned to civilization physically sound. Only your memory will be missing. A relatively simple leucotomy will erase all this – and, indeed, all your past life – from your brain. When you are recovered, I'll have you flown home to the London Hospital for Diseases of the Nervous System. Poor Dr Pilgrim, they will say, he's nothing but a vegetable despite everything Stromberg could do.

'As for you, mademoiselle, I have other plans. I have a penchant for women with beautiful hair . . . and soon I shall need a new source. . . .' He turned to the two Haitians lounging by the door. 'Henri!' he called.

One straightened and swaggered past the coffin and walked towards Peter. Before Peter could move, he whipped out a leather-bound cosh and, with the expertise gained as a terrorist agent, swung it against the side of his head. Peter's knees buckled and he collapsed to the floor.

23

A few minutes after Peter was struck to the floor he opened his eyes. Although he suffered from pain down the side of his head and a feeling of nausea, his mind was quite able to comprehend what was happening.

He was on his back, his arms and legs tightly pinioned by straps to a narrow table. Light poured down on him from an adjustable non-dazzling lamp such as are used in operating theatres. By turning his head he saw the walls were made of gleaming hygienic tiles. There was a familiar smell in the air, and when Dr Stromberg moved into his line of sight he saw he was gowned in white.

'What's happening?' he asked weakly.

'I'm preparing you for your operation,' Stromberg answered. 'I regret facilities are very primitive for such surgery, but to operate in the clinic theatre would excite suspicion among the staff. Here, unfortunately, I only have this examination room at my disposal, but you can appreciate that what I intend to do is relatively crude compared to usual brain surgery.'

Peter said nothing.

'I also regret that I do not have an anaesthetist whom I could trust,' he continued. 'You will have the interesting experience of actually feeling the probe. Now, Miss Saturday....'

Swivelling his eyes, Peter saw the feline Haitian girl looking down at him with concentration. She began to cut away the hair from his forehead with scissors. It hurt when hairs caught between the blades.

'You can't do this,' Peter shouted. 'It's utter madness.'

'I assure you of my best professional attention,' said Stromberg. 'The instruments are correctly sterilized, and I am sure Mademoiselle Clair will give you the best of post-surgical care. I did ask her to help me with the theatre work, but she was uncooperative. Saturday may be eager, but her experience is negligible.'

As he spoke tufts of hair continued to fall into Peter's eyes. When sufficient had been removed, he saw black hands moving above his face as his stubbly scalp was lathered prior to being shaved.

From somewhere behind his head came the buzz of a delicate electric drill. Experience told him Stromberg was testing the device which would bore the preliminary aperture in his skull.

It was then that Peter lost control. His throat seemed to open of its own will and he heard his continuous scream fill the room.

'Please, doctor, I have not touched you yet,' chided Stromberg, switching off his drill. 'You must appreciate that such a noise could upset my concentration at a delicate moment. Perhaps I should inject some nova into your throat muscles to ensure your silence.'

Tears rolled from Peter's eyes and he could not control his sobbing. Detailed knowledge of what was to come robbed him of all dignity and fortitude. He felt warmth round his loins as the fear gripping his nervous system caused micturition.

Uselessly he turned his head from side to side, then heard Stromberg giving directions to his guards for putting a head clamp in place. The urine dripping from the table caused them to joke in Haitian-French patois.

'Time to wash up now,' said Stromberg, and disappeared from Peter's vision. The Tontons followed, and he was left alone with the stink of his sweat.

A minute passed – the longest minute in Peter's life. Somewhere an alarm bell clattered. It was followed by shouts echoing down the corridor – harsh sounds of command and obedience. Then there was a long silence during which Peter struggled to master the terror which had robbed him of reason.

Where was Anne-Marie? he wondered. What would Bruno do when the scheduled transmissions did not come through?

From a long way off came the rumble of engines breaking into life, followed by the sharp crack of a rifle. Peter had no idea what was happening, but found himself laughing with hysterical relief as he realized that, for the moment at least, Stromberg's glittering instruments would not slide into the soft centre of his being.

He was still chuckling when Bruno ran through the door and cursed in shrill Italian at the sight of his friend with the front of his head shaved like a clown.

'I came with the Lapps,' muttered Bruno in explanation as he fumbled with the straps holding Peter to the examination table. 'Stromberg and his gang have taken off in the *Vlad*, and they've got Holly and Anne-Marie with them. Come on, doctor, get up and say something to me.'

'I've wet myself,' confessed Peter, sitting up shakily and rubbing the newly bald part of his skull. Tears of relief ran down his face and Bruno, with great gentleness, wiped them away with a stained handkerchief.

'Never mind that, we must get out of here,' he said. 'Uutsi and his boys are going to level this place.'

Peter stood up.

'I'm all right now,' he said though he still trembled. As

Bruno helped him out of the room and down the corridor, he asked what had happened.

Tersely Bruno explained how Uutsi's raiding party had come in three Lapp boats. At the approach of the armed men Stromberg had boarded the *Vlad*, his Tontons bringing the two prisoners. Saturday was at the wheel as the cruiser raced from the island.

'I can't believe he'll abandon his chapel,' Peter said as they came out of the windowless block. 'It's his spiritual home.'

Outside he saw the three Lapp boats, like scaled-down Viking ships with heavy outboards at their sterns, beached in the bay opposite the annexe. A group of blue-costumed men clustered round the big fuel tank, while on rocks overlooking the bay a man in a leather jacket stood watching the Fjord standing-to at a safe distance.

Bruno took Peter over to Uutsi.

'This is my friend,' he said. 'He will tell you everything your wisemen have said about Stromberg is true. He has not a man's spirit.'

Uutsi nodded, then pointed to the *Vlad*. Its engines suddenly roared at full throttle and two high crests of foam surged from its bows as it headed straight for the island. Crouching at the pulpit rail the Tonton called Henri held a Thompson submachine gun.

As the cruiser raced towards the bay, the muzzle of the gun began to flash and a swathe of bullets swept the shore. A Lapp gave a cry and fell as his companions dived for cover behind granite rocks. Ricocheting bullets whined over Peter's head as he flattened himself behind the trunk of a dead tree.

'No wonder he took to his boat when he had a machine gun aboard,' cried Bruno beside him. Seizing his .22, he began firing with the Lapps at the speeding craft.

The *Vlad* continued to bear down on the bay as though it

was going to smash itself against the rocks. At the last moment Saturday spun the wheel and reversed the port engine. The craft made a turn so tight its wake crashed against the shore like a miniature tidal wave and set the Lapp boats bucking wildly.

For the few seconds the *Vlad* was broadside on the second Tonton opened up with another machine gun. Chips of wood flew high in the air above Peter's bulwark. At the water's edge one of the Lapp boats was practically cut in two with the relentless stream of nickel-plated lead. Then the cruiser sped away with a zig-zagging course to avoid the Lapps' bullets.

Peter shouted: 'Stop firing! They've got hostages aboard!' Uutsi heard him and gave a command in his own language. Reluctantly the rifle fire died.

Peering over the bullet-scarred trunk, Peter saw Anne-Marie crouching in the stern of the *Vlad*. Stromberg, a pistol in his hand, stood beside Saturday on the helmsman's platform. The two Haitians fitted new drums, each containing fifty rounds, to their Tommy guns ready for the next attack.

Suddenly Anne-Marie straightened up and dived into the foaming wake of the cruiser.

'Oh God,' moaned Peter. 'They'll pick her off in the water.'

Next instant he saw the reason for her action. Flames fountained skywards from the cockpit. Stromberg and Saturday turned and gazed in horror at the inferno, then they vanished as jerrycans of petrol burst and enveloped the whole craft in a blinding sheet of white fire.

Bruno cried out as a figure was briefly silhouetted against the blazing curtain before it fell like a burning doll into the steaming water. With the twin Volvos making thunder, the *Vlad* left a trail of flame and black smoke as it careered in a crazy circle before the main fuel tanks exploded. It disintegrated in a blast which echoed across the face of Lake Inari. Seconds later all that was left were blazing fragments floating lazily through the smoky air.

A couple of Lapps started an outboard and, after Bruno and Peter leapt aboard, headed at full speed to where Anne-Marie could be seen swimming strongly towards the island. Soon Peter was helping her over the side. Her chest heaved as she fought to regain her breath.

'It was Holly,' she gasped. 'When the shooting started they were too busy to notice what she was doing. She unscrewed the cap from an extra can so petrol poured into the cockpit. When I saw her take out her lighter I knew what was coming and went over the stern.'

With the outboard at half-speed the Lapps circled until one called out. The motor was cut and the boat drifted alongside a floating body. It was Holly, a long piece of chain still fastened to her wrist.

Tenderly Bruno lifted her aboard, and Peter said: 'I'm afraid she's dead, Bruno.' The Italian nodded, took off his bush jacket and laid it over the face of the woman he had loved so briefly. As the boat sped back to the island, he spoke quietly to Peter and after a minute Peter nodded slowly.

Uutsi came forward as the Lapp boat ran its high prow on to the pebbled beach.

'This is a hell business,' he cried. 'One man dead and three wounded. Doctor, will you have a look at them, then be ready to leave. We will run fuel oil into the cellar and leave a fuse to set ablaze. When the authorities investigate they'll think it was an accident and the boat caught fire at the same time.'

'In that case you'd better get your men to pick up their used cartridge cases,' said Peter. Bruno carried Holly's body into the small building where the diesel generator was still supplying power to illuminate Stromberg's chapel. With Anne-

Marie helping him with makeshift bandages, Peter began his first aid work.

'Now we know the truth about Stromberg I must do something about the children Britt attacked when I get back to England,' Peter muttered as he bent over a Lapp whose groans were checked by fiercely gritted teeth. 'Somehow I must get them segregated . . . Oh God, even with Stromberg truly dead at last, Britt can pass on the curse.'

'Britt is dead, too,' Anne-Marie said. 'When I was taken aboard the boat I saw her in the cabin, lying on one of the bunks. Perhaps Stromberg had been afraid to leave her alone with the staff. She would not have felt anything, she was in her trance.'

When Peter had done what he could for the wounded, Uutsi said: 'We must go quickly. We will take you to Bruno's camp, then we will head north. For the next few weeks we will be in Finnmark on a big reindeer drive. We will be most surprised when the news of this disaster reaches us!'

'Give me a few minutes. There is something I have to do,' Peter said.

He ran into the main building where a flexible fuel pipe was flooding the crypt with oil. In the room where so shortly before he had met and succumbed to fear he wrenched open a sterile cabinet, snatching a scalpel and a surgical saw.

Outside again, he strode to the generator room where, beside the vibrating machinery, the body of Holly was laid on the cement floor. He pulled Bruno's jacket from the distorted face and knelt down.

Afterwards he sometimes wondered if the greenish eyes had opened fractionally as he began the dissection.

They were exhausted when they reached the camouflaged Citroën. Anne-Marie, who had changed into some of Bruno's spare clothes when the Lapps landed them near his camp, sank into the back seat with a moan of weariness.

Peter, with his face unnaturally strained, helped Bruno pull away the pine branches which covered the car. A dry stick tore the skin above his elbow but in his haste the pain was unnoticed.

Bruno was silent. He frequently glanced at his watch, waiting for Uutsi's primitive fuse to ignite the oil which by now filled the crypt. Suddenly the wind brought the thud of a detonation. The Lapland sun was almost touching the horizon, and they saw a pillar of smoke soar against the crimson backdrop.

'We must get away quickly,' said Bruno, sliding behind the wheel. Through the trees came a distant howling – a lament from the wolves who had been congregating in the Inari forest. Peter climbed in the back beside a quiet Anne-Marie.

Bruno started the engine, the Citroën rose on its hydraulic suspension and reversed over the soft forest floor to the road which curved away to the south.

'It's all over,' Peter said. 'But at the moment I cannot take in what's happened.'

'Yes, everything's over,' Bruno agreed automatically.

Peter turned to the girl with the pale gold hair beside him.

'We'll forget this together,' he murmured. 'When will you be free to marry me, Anne-Marie?'

But she was not listening to him. Her violet eyes were hypnotized by the thick trickle of blood which welled from the cut on his arm.